A Delicate Seduction

A Harwell Heirs Legacy Romance

Harwell Heirs Book 4

Regina Kammer

Viridium Press

Copyright ©2023 by Regina Kammer
Special fonts: Nymphette by Lauren Thompson, Ships Font by Sassy Graphics
Cover design: Dar Albert, Wicked Smart Designs

Published by: Viridium Press, Friday Harbor, Washington
ISBN-13: (paperback) 978-0-9978893-9-0
ISBN-10: (paperback) 0-9978893-9-X
ISBN-13: (ebook) 978-0-9978893-8-3
ISBN-10: (ebook) 0-9978893-8-1

The Harwell Heirs

Victorian aristocracy has very strict rules concerning marital connections and familial obligations. But the Harwell heirs—Helena, Sophia, and Arthur—discover love doesn't always follow the rules. Scandalous affairs force these scions of society to choose between duty and desire, deference and destiny.

Book 1: *The Pleasure Device*

Book 2: *Disobedience By Design*

Book 3: *Where Destiny Plays*

***Harwell Heirs* Legacy Romances**

Travel beyond England's shores for these stories featuring beloved secondary characters from the first three books of the series. The Legacy novels delve into the romances of the friends, family, and intimates of the extended Harwell family.

Book 4: *A Delicate Seduction*

Book 5: *Discovering Her Delight*

Book 6: *Their Noble Deceit*

Acknowledgments & Content Note

Thank you to Corey Alexander and their insights on writing characters who are trauma survivors. Corey's work was a resource for this novel.

Content note: The character of Percival Wood, the Marquess of Norrington, is a survivor of intimate partner violence. The abuse happened prior to the timeline of this novel, and is not described overtly on page. However, past abuse is referenced, and some situations trigger Percival's memories.

Dedication

To my father.

CHAPTER ONE

Dastardly fellows, they were, those who preyed on the
unsuspecting and innocent. As for the latter, they required a hero, a
protector, a champion.
— *The Adventures of Paolo the Pirate Hunter*

St. Albans, Hertfordshire, May 1879

Jack is dead.

Percival Wood, the Marquess of Norrington, had to remind
himself of that fact as his carriage approached the Atherley manor
house. Jonathan Atherley, the Viscount Saxondale, known as "Jack
of Diamonds" by his wastrel friends, was dead, his body buried
deep in the ground. Percival had absolutely nothing to fear.

So why was his heart pounding under shivering flesh, his
lungs so tight he could scarcely breathe?

Because the torments his former lover had inflicted still
terrified, the scars still burned. Even after three years, the tattered
shreds of memories continued to haunt him.

Perhaps one day Percival would be able to erase those memories. Perhaps one day there would be a hero to supplant the villain. But only if Percival could gather the courage to even allow another man anywhere near his heart.

Or his body.

He shuddered.

The wheels of the brougham crunched along the gravel drive, every revolution dragging him closer to inevitability. The clip-clop of horse hooves added a menacing beat to his already rattled nerves.

The Earl of St. Albans, the lord of Atherley manor, had summoned Percival. Father had called Percival back from Oxford and had advised he see the earl as swiftly as possible to make peace with his past.

Father had also insisted two burly and imposing footmen accompany Percival in the event Jack's dissolute friends decided to pay the earl a visit at the same time.

What Father didn't know was that once Jack had spent all his money, his equally profligate friends had abandoned him. Most likely the only people present at the Atherley manor would be the dying earl and his trusty manservant Mason.

The brougham stopped before the Gothic edifice, the pale yellow stone a greenish-gray from mildew and neglect. One of the footmen opened the carriage door and helped Percival alight.

"Shall I accompany you to the entrance, my lord?"

Percival let out a tremulous exhalation. "Thank you. No."

The footman bowed in understanding.

As he approached the entry porch, Percival's gut churned. He paused to square his shoulders before resuming his path. He could not let Jack—or rather, the ghost of Jack—continue to hector him. He absolutely had to conquer his fears. He stared straight ahead at the entrance portal taking renewed interest in the delicate arches over slim columns, finding such grace and elegance at odds with the violence that had taken place within.

Once at the door, he turned the bell, the sound almost nostalgic.

The gray-haired Mason answered, his eyes widening upon recognition, briefly disturbing his otherwise stoic countenance. "My lord Norrington. What a pleasure." He waved him into the Great Hall.

"The pleasure is mine, Mason." The butler had always been a kind soul. "Is the earl receiving visitors?"

"He is. He will be delighted to see you." He gestured to the staircase. "If you will follow me, my lord."

"Thank you."

Mason led the way. "Lord Saxondale is here, as well."

An ominous chill stopped Percival cold. Had the ghost returned? "Lord Saxondale?"

The butler turned, all color drained from his face. "Pardon me, my lord marquess," he murmured. "The new Lord Saxondale. Master Nicholas Atherley."

Relief drenched him. Nicky. Jack's younger brother and, by far, his better. "Thank you, Mason. I'm certain Nicholas and I have a great deal to discuss."

A flush re-colored the butler's pallor. "Of course."

As they climbed stairs and traversed corridors, nothing seemed changed. Portraits still hung on paneled walls, furniture remained unmoved. Yet everything had changed. The deafening silence was evidence of that. No hum of servants, no raucous antics of Jack and his friends, no cheery melodies sung by the countess—

Percival's heart clenched.

The Countess of St. Albans had been a second mother to him, had protected him. Had been killed trying to save him from Jack's drunken wrath.

He shook his head, trying to dislodge the demons.

Mason stopped before the door to the countess's summer morning room, a place filled with pleasant memories. Percival raised an eyebrow in his direction.

"The bedroom wing was closed after—" Mason stopped, his expression pensive for a moment. "After you no longer came to visit us."

After the death of the countess.

"I understand." Percival sucked in a breath.

Mason hesitated, hand on the knob. "Are you ready, my lord?"

"I think so." Yet his head spun. He wasn't ready. He stilled Mason's hand. "No."

The butler regarded him with sympathetic eyes.

"What can I expect? The earl was shot—" by Jack "—where? I mean, where on his person?" There was only so much gruesome horror he could take.

"St. Albans was shot above the heart. He is bedridden, and much changed because of the incident. There was an infection."

"Oh."

"Master Nicholas is a doctor now. He has attended to the wound and has done what he can to make his father comfortable."

"Thank you, Mason. I think I am ready."

Mason knocked on the door before entering, holding up a hand to forestall Percival. "My lord," he called into the room, "the Marquess of Norrington is here to see you."

"Norrington?" queried a feeble, gravelly voice. "Ah, yes, Percy. Percy! Come here, my boy."

Mason waved Percival inside, then left, closing the door behind him.

Before the fireplace was positioned a small cot upon which lay a sallow and wrinkled old man overwhelmed by a goose-down counterpane.

Percival swallowed the lump of disbelief that formed in his throat.

Three years ago the Earl of St. Albans had been hale and booming, a formidable presence in the Atherley house. He'd had to be in order to keep Jack in line.

"Pull up a chair, Percy. Come sit by me."

The kind invitation warmed his muscles numbed by shock. "Yes, my lord." He grabbed a side chair and placed it at the head of the cot.

"Oh, pshaw. You used to call me Papa Robert."

The memory educed a grin. "I did. And the countess, Mama Louisa."

"But you don't care for such foolishness anymore, do you?"

"It's simply been a long time since I've seen you, Papa Robert."

"And much tragedy," St. Albans croaked. He smiled, crinkles framing the spark now returned in his brown eyes. "You were a fine boy, Percy. You've become a handsome man."

Heat rose in Percival's face. "Thank you."

"Except there is a sternness that mars your brow."

The flush dissipated. No one had ever said that to him. Probably no one had ever noticed. But St. Albans—Papa Robert— would perceive and understand the change in him.

"I had hoped, had prayed, you would save Jack from himself," continued the earl. "I had thought, foolishly it seems, your innocence and admiration for him would change him. Would show him the way of love."

Percival's pulse pounded in his ears.

"I know the power of love. Louisa was almost able to change me. I regret it was not she who did so, but, instead, the final act of violence by my accursed son."

Percival's eyes burned with unshed tears.

"I'm sorry, Percy. I truly am. I did not realize Jack had been monstrous to you. Louisa's death revealed so much to my willful obliviousness."

Percival's face ached from restraint.

"He hurt you. I know that now. But he learned that from me. I hurt Louisa. God, how I regret my behavior."

Lightheadedness descended. He had to breathe, breathe, *breathe*.

"You must forgive me, Percy. You can damn Jack all the way to hell, but I need your forgiveness." A frail hand slid from under the coverlet and touched Percival's knee, fingers reaching for more. "Please."

Percival grasped the earl's hand. A wave of emotion overpowered him, unleashing tears and sobs.

"Oh, Papa Robert, I don't know if I can trust again, if I can love again." Percival turned away to hide his tears.

"You will learn, son." The earl gave his hand a faint squeeze. "You have to. So Louisa will not have died in vain. I know love exists within you. I've seen it. There is someone out there who is worthy of it."

Percival wiped his eyes with his handkerchief.

"Percy, my boy, don't let Jack steal your happiness. Defeat him. You have a lifetime ahead of you. Open yourself to love."

"I'll try, Papa Robert." He would, he really would. He *had* tried. But it was proving to be very difficult.

"Love is all that matters in this world." A squeeze again, this time with more energy. "Take some advice from a dying man, Percy."

Percival clung to the earl as the emotion and tears he had been holding back came like a flood to overwhelm him.

BERTRAM ATHERLEY, the Viscount Ravensburgh, sat on a weathered boulder to observe the dilapidated stone edifice that was the gatehouse to a once-grand estate. The iron gate itself was long gone. A sparsely covered gravel drive led to the ancestral home of the Earls of St. Albans, surname Atherley. The large manor, in the Gothic style, was also known, simply, as Uncle Robert's house.

And Uncle Robert was on his deathbed.

A pang of sorrow threatened to unleash tears, but was quickly vanquished. By now, at the ripe old age of twenty-eight, Bertram was practiced in the art of repressing such emotions. He'd been thrust into the role of viscount as a mere boy of five upon the death of his father. Soon Uncle Robert would be joining Papa in heaven. He was certain of that.

But cousin Jack was surely already festering in hell.

The thought brought on a smug smile, quickly dulled by the realization that his connections to the past were fracturing like the crumbling estate before him.

Bertram stood, stretching his spine and filling his lungs. Time to see his uncle and glean the last bits of family memories from the dying man.

Melancholia swiftly turned to happy surprise when he espied a carriage in the drive, its door emblazoned with a familiar coat-of-arms. The blue shield and gold cross supported by stags rampant was the unmistakable crest of the Duke of Amesbury.

So someone else was here reconciling with the past. And that someone—most assuredly the Duke of Amesbury's heir, Percival Wood, the Marquess of Norrington—had quite a bit of reconciling to do.

Two brawny footmen leaned against the brougham looking a little bored, probably wondering why there were no groomsmen to attend the horses and no maid offering tea. Clearly Percival had been with Uncle Robert for a while already.

Well, he'd give him a little while longer. The reunion between Uncle Robert and Percival was most likely profoundly emotional.

Bertram sat on the boulder again, sorrow waxing into nostalgia. As a youth, he had played on the grounds of the estate with cousin Nicholas and Percival—then called Percy—whose unfettered boyish imagination for inventing new games had provoked boundless amusement for all three of them.

The Duke of Amesbury had indulged his son, giving him considerable freedom. Percy had taken advantage of that freedom by using the nearby Atherley estate as his playground. The boy liked the unkempt wildness of the land versus the well-maintained Amesbury garden trimmed in the French geometric style. Little did

Percy know that the Earl of St. Albans was too deep in debt to afford a full panoply of gardeners and groundskeepers and, hence, neglected his garden.

But once Percy grew to be a strapping youth, and Jack had seduced him into a world of debauchery and gambling, Percy must have got an inkling of the reason behind the crumbling stone and overgrown weeds.

Bertram sighed.

He knew exactly what Jack had seen in Percy. An innocence and *joie de vivre* that one loses once the responsibilities of manhood loom. But Jack ended up destroying those very qualities in Percy that Jack—and Bertram—had cherished.

Regret prickled within despite knowing there wasn't anything Bertram could have done. He, along with cousin Nicholas, had been away at university when it first happened. They simply had no idea.

Jack had swooped in while Percy was in his adolescence, a beastly thing to do.

Bertram had grown suspicious after he'd attempted a correspondence with Percy—now called Norrington, his courtesy title. Norrington's responses had been erratic, too frequently using illness or fatigue as an excuse for not writing earlier, and when pressed as to what ailed him, always providing an ambiguous answer.

Rumor in the village was that the young marquess was frequently in the company of Jack and his profligate friends.

What the villagers did not know was Jack was quick to anger, especially when he got drunk, and Norrington was in danger. When Bertram had confronted Jack, he'd been met with terrifying rage behind the barrel of a gun.

Not too long after that day, Aunt Louisa had been killed trying to save Norrington from Jack, and Norrington was quickly whisked away by his father and quietly tucked into the depths of Oxford.

After an impassioned request to the Duke of Amesbury, Bertram was granted permission to resume his correspondence with Norrington. With every letter, Bertram fell deeper into an infatuation for his boyhood friend.

He never told him. Of course not. Their friendship was paramount. Norrington absolutely did not need yet another older Atherley man attempting seduction.

His intentions with their exchange of letters had been virtuous…at first. He'd been thinking of writing a novel for adventurous boys such as Norrington had once been and wanted the marquess's advice. The novel involved a pirate and a pirate hunter. As time had passed, the metaphors revealed themselves to be reflective of reality.

Bertram had wanted to stop those who preyed on young innocents. Especially since the innocent had become an object of affection and physical attraction for himself.

A deep inhalation helped tether Bertram back to the present. His slow exhalation scattered painful thoughts of the past.

Percival had surely had enough time with Uncle Robert. Bertram climbed down from the rocks limning the estate and approached the front entrance, avoiding the bored footmen.

He rang the doorbell then took a step back as he waited.

Moments later, the door opened revealing the stalwart butler Mason.

Mason's countenance brightened. "Master Bertram." His eyes were bloodshot, his voice unsteady. "Pardon me, my lord viscount."

Heartache choked Bertram's lungs. He swallowed hard. Mason's immediately calling him by his boyhood name revealed tomes about the old butler's emotional state.

"Hello, Mason. I am here to see my uncle."

Mason stepped aside to let Bertram enter.

"My lord, you are welcome at the manor. However, I fear the earl's visit with the Marquess of Norrington has taxed his lordship's energy. He has fallen asleep. I am not sure when he will awaken."

Bertram's gut clenched. "But he will awaken, won't he?"

Mason paled. "Oh, yes, most certainly so. He is simply tired." He lowered his voice. "The hour is not yet come."

Bertram exhaled.

"My lord, I suggest you stay for tea in the meantime."

"Thank you, Mason. Am I correct in assuming the Marquess of Norrington is still here?"

"Yes. He is taking a stroll after his visit. The new Lord Saxondale is about, as well." Mason lowered his voice. "Meaning Master Nicholas."

"Then I'll wander the grounds until I find one or both of them. I'll return later to see if my uncle is awake."

"Very good, sir." Something akin to a smile played upon Mason's lips.

"And if not today, then tomorrow. I'll return tomorrow. The cottage is not so very far, and I enjoy the walk."

Sadness lingered in Mason's eyes, an indiscretion most loyal and experienced servants would seek to mask. "The earl would love to see you, Master Bertram. Today or tomorrow. Or both."

"And I would love to see my uncle. Please, if possible, prepare him for my visit. I hope to hear stories about my father."

"Your father George was a fine man and a patriot." Mason cleared his throat. "I will make sure the earl has stories to tell."

Bertram left the obviously distraught butler to explore whatever adventure, involving the past or present, awaited him on the estate.

PERCIVAL WALKED THE GROUNDS he once trod upon as a child. He knew the topography intimately, every rock, every tree, every hillock. Yet the vista from the boulder upon which he used to play was very much changed. Overgrowth now shrouded the rolling hills. The landscape had never been as perfectly trimmed as his home at Wood Hall, but former hiding places offering fodder for imagination were now tangles of weeds even the most intrepid boy would not venture to play in.

A figure approached. Male. Dark hair, tall, the bounce of youth still in his step. As he came closer his smile widened in recognition.

And Percival's smile did too. His boyhood friend Nicholas Atherley was a fine sight to behold. He resembled a kinder version of his elder brother Jack.

"Nicky!"

Nicholas quickened his step, grasping Percival's hands when face to face, then flinging his arms around him in a vigorous hug.

"Percy, so wonderful to see you. Mason said you were visiting." Nicholas drew back surveying Percival from head to toe. "How grown you are."

"It's been ten years since last we met."

"I suppose it has," Nicholas said thoughtfully. "Quite a bit has happened in the meantime." He motioned they should continue their stroll.

"Have you just returned from your sojourn with the Ottomans?"

Nicholas chuckled weakly. "I returned last winter. I felt it time to pursue my profession and be a proper Englishman."

"Ah, yes, I hear you are a doctor now. And that Papa Robert was recently one of your patients."

Nicholas stopped to gape with glistening eyes. "You used to call him that, didn't you?" He wiped a tear. "I've had some heartfelt discussions with him. I grieve that it's taken such a tragedy to enable us to be cordial to each other. To be a family again."

"How does he feel about you being Doctor Atherley?"

"Ah, well, first of all, I'm Doctor Ramsay. I took Mama's maiden name when I left for the East. To honor her. Papa understands."

"Now that you've reconciled, will you change your name again?"

"I don't know." Nicholas's smile faded. "I hadn't considered it."

"Well, you may soon be the Earl of St. Albans instead."

"I can't… I don't want to think about that now." Nicholas pursed his lips as his gaze seared with an eerie intensity. "Percy, I just learned… You see, I burned most of the letters from home unopened. I didn't know… I mean, I knew about my brother, how he was…. And I knew you spent a great deal of time here…" A crinkle formed above his nose. "I just did not know the true nature of your relationship with Jack."

Percival chilled. "And are you outraged by the indecency of it?"

"What?" Nicholas paled. "Good God, no." He shook his head. "I don't care about…*that*. I *do* care that you were abused, and I feel…" He sighed heavily. "I feel as if I should have stayed."

"Whatever for?"

"I could have saved Mama. I could have saved you."

"Now that you're a doctor, you can save all sorts of people."

"Percy, don't be so flippant."

"Nicky, I admit some scars will be difficult to heal. Being here…" He looked around at the landscape. "I feel the stinging pain of those scars more deeply. But you had to leave. You were abused as well. And Jack might have killed you, instead."

"I would give my life to have my mother back amongst the living."

"No, no, no. Mama Louisa wanted you to flourish, live, be happy. She talked about you often, Nicky. She understood why you left. She loved you."

Nicholas shook his head as a pallor dulled his expression. "I was a coward for leaving her."

"Jack was the coward for not controlling his emotions. For not controlling his drinking. For not realizing his fair-weather friends were not friends at all."

Nicholas beamed. "So wise for one so young."

"Well, my father did send me to Oxford to contemplate my existence."

That elicited a guffaw. Nicholas patted Percival on the shoulder. "And what conclusions have you drawn?"

"That I need to contemplate my existence not in a cloister. I'm planning a Grand Tour. Well, perhaps not so grand, really. Italy, most assuredly. Perhaps some beaches along the Mediterranean coast for their meditative vistas. I need to put some distance between my old life and what I wish my life to be."

"That sounds marvelous."

"I have yet to convince my father of the notion."

Nicholas shuffled his feet. "Now that Jack is no longer a threat, I'm sure the duke will allow your freedom."

"Nicky, my father doesn't know about the affair with Jack."

"What?" Nicholas was genuinely surprised. "But I thought he sent you to Oxford to get away from him."

"From Jack's drinking and gambling, yes. Father doesn't know about our physical relationship."

"Oh."

"He hopes I'll find a pretty girl of some venerable European aristocratic bloodline and settle down." Percival sighed. "But I'm not entirely sure I want a girl, even a pretty one. In fact, I am certain I do not. Mostly such an arrangement would not be fair to the girl."

Nicholas's grin reflected the sincerity of his emotion. Nothing like the deceptive artifice of his brother. "You have plenty of time, Percy. I can't believe the duke would expect you to marry at only twenty-one. Why, Amesbury is a man in the height of his vigor. You're not succeeding him any time soon."

"Yes, but, succeed him I must one day, and, as society expects, with a duchess at my side. For the moment, marriage is a prospect I do not want to think about. Not when I have so much on my mind already."

"While marriage is on my mind too much of late."

Percival's jaw dropped. "Nicky? Are you getting married?"

"Ah, no. I'm just of an age, and, with establishing my profession, well, I think it's time. You know, as society expects."

Percival clapped him on the shoulder. "Well, if the happy event occurs soon, you must promise you will call me back from the continent. Mother will know how to contact me."

Nicholas blushed. "Of course, Percy."

"I must fly. Mother wants me to meet with a French tailor, I suppose to make me look presentable should I encounter French aristocrats on my holiday. So wonderful to see you, Nicky. Write me of your marriage prospects and I'll write back of the golden sun on the shores of the Mediterranean."

Their parting with a hearty hug left Percival with a warm glow, a sense that he had reconnected with family again. He walked briskly in the direction of the gravel drive and his awaiting brougham. Tromping down a rocky mound he spied a man near the entrance portal.

A man with the same unruly brown hair, the same height, the same fine features of the Atherley sons.

Because Bertram Atherley, the Second Viscount Ravensburgh, was cousin to Nicky and Jack.

And the best friend Percival had ever had.

That warm feeling sparked in his heart again, that same joy-filled nostalgia, but this time with a bit of a difference. What that difference was, he couldn't say. Bertram simply made him feel happy, excited, and worthy.

Mother would just have to keep her French tailor waiting.

~ INTERLUDE ~

The Adventures of Paolo the Pirate Hunter, the Magnificent Adventurer, who, along with his First Mate Barnaby, Protects the Seas from the Evil Pirate Jonas the Marauder

by Bertram Atherley, The Right Honorable 2nd Viscount Ravensburgh

"Land ho, my captain!"

Paolo whipped his gaze from the incessant horizon to his trusty first mate Barnaby and held out his hand.

Barnaby clapped the spyglass in his palm. Paolo squinted through the lens, finding the mountainous rise of Tortuga quickly.

"Make haste! All hands on deck!"

Intelligence and determination had set them upon the sea, winds from the east billowing their sails from New Providence to

Tortuga. A pirate had absconded to the island, taking refuge in the old hill fort, terrorizing the inhabitants who had exiled themselves to the abandoned port town trying to eke out an existence from the remnants of illicit glories past.

The winds blew favorably as they rounded the western tip, yet, upon reaching the strait, Fortune stilled Zephyr's breath until only a trifling puff danced upon the canvas. The crew willed the *Georgius* forward, mustering strength as they pulled ropes, straining muscles as they encouraged the sails to catch the inconstant breeze.

The port lay in their sights, maddeningly close, yet still so far away. If only they had oars to propel them—

A tremendous explosion ripped through the wharf, inciting crewmen to crouch on the deck, shooting splinters of wood into the air, shattering the surface of the cerulean sea.

Death blighted the scene—the land, the water, filled with the bodies of men killed in a wanton act of destruction. Men innocent of their assassin, innocent of his intent. Men who may not have been entirely free of sin, but who did not deserve unprovoked execution. Only God Himself could save them now.

"Halt!" Paolo commanded his crew. Instantly, all activity ceased.

Suddenly, Fortune freed Zephyr to beat his wings, aiding them toward calmer seas and a natural harbor. There they dropped anchor. With a handful of men, Paolo and Barnaby alighted on the pinnace and rowed to shore.

A somber mood silenced conversation, but Paolo and his shipmates knew their purpose. They would go help those left behind, those who survived the unimaginable tragedy.

Once aid had been delivered to the victims, then Paolo would turn his attention to the villain who had committed such horror.

~ * ~ * ~ * ~

CHAPTER TWO

For a voyage, a seasoned, capable crew was essential. But an adventure required a best mate at one's side.
— *The Adventures of Paolo the Pirate Hunter*

"Bertie!"

Bertram turned at the familiar voice. Percival rushed toward him, waving, hat in hand, the unmistakable shock of blond hair bouncing with each step.

A grin was inexorable. He could never contain happiness when Percival was about.

He also could not contain the spark of desire that burst forth upon seeing his friend-turned-fantasy in the flesh. His burgeoning arousal threatened to rend his drawers. He removed his own hat to cover the evidence, then attempted to calm his wandering mind and contumacious body.

Percival threw his arms around him, breaking any concentration he had.

Bollocks.

He simply stopped trying to control the libidinous sensations rioting within. Percival had such an effect on him. He only hoped the marquess did not notice the peculiar placement of his hat. Being at Atherley manor must be distressing for Percival. Now was not the time for a sensual encounter.

"I hadn't even imagined you might be here," Percival said as he drew back. "How fortuitous."

Bertram cleared the lust in his throat. "It is so good to see you, Percy. Despite the circumstances."

"And I just got your letter not two days ago."

His heart skipped a beat. "Oh? Did you enjoy the story?"

"I did," Percival said with a chuckle. "It seems Paolo the Pirate Hunter is quite clever."

"Of course he is. He's the hero. He's supposed to be clever."

Percival sulked. "I wish I could be so clever." He met Bertram's gaze. "I dare say it was difficult seeing St. Albans in his weakened state." He swiped his fingers over his eyes. "God, look at me crying like a boy."

Bertram placed a hand on Percival's shoulder, tamping down the ardor that flared even with the gentle, concern-laden touch. "You've returned to a place of painful memories, Percy. It is to be expected. We cannot exert control at every moment of the day." Bertram's prick was proof of that. "And you're probably feeling quite a turmoil of emotions."

"Seeing Papa Robert shriveled and in pain was positively wrenching to my heart."

"Percy, it isn't just that."

"How do you mean?"

"Jack's death must seem a great relief despite the tragedy."

Percival looked askance. "Yes. I'll admit that I've been set free of a horrible burden. And I won't have to hide at Oxford anymore."

"Hide? Everyone knew you were at Oxford. Presumably even Jack."

"Of course. But my rooms at Corpus Christi are tucked away on the uppermost floor. And Father has a guard posted at night."

Bertram uttered an oath through his teeth.

"At least the guard is not obvious as such. He plays the part of an older student in the room next to mine. I suspect some of my fellow students are in Father's employ, as well. I hope they are availing themselves of the lectures at least."

"Will you be returning to Oxford?"

Percival pressed his lips together. "I left early because of…this. I'm postponing my exams until Michaelmas term. Right now, I have a mind to go to the continent."

"The continent? Where?"

"I intend to explore ruins in Italy, then venture along the Mediterranean coast to gloriously sunny places where I can forget England's dreary drizzle."

Bertram laughed. "That will be a change."

"Warm sea breezes will be good for my world-weary heart and soul." He sighed. "I'll visit museums and cafés and stroll along sandy beaches ogling fishermen." A mischievous glint glimmered in Percival's eye. "Come with me."

Desire flared anew, awakening every pore. "To Italy?"

"And the Mediterranean coast—" Percival stopped abruptly, then shook his head. "Oh, God, Bertie, I apologize. This must seem like I'm propositioning you."

"Percy, no, it does not—"

"I know you know about me. Of course you do. My own father has no idea. But the Atherleys know all about Jack and his inverted ways."

Bertram grunted. "I despise that word."

Percival raised his brows. "You *know* that word?"

"Of course I do. What with Jack being as such and me being a member of the Atherley family."

It took a moment for Percival to grasp the dark joke. He chuckled.

"But, yes, Percy, I do know that word. All who are inverted know that word."

Percival started, then paled. "You?"

Bertram bowed. "Molly at your service, my lord."

"You never told me."

"Do I need to remind you that such inclinations are punishable by life imprisonment? What if someone had found one of my letters?"

"But...but if you...and Jack..." His eyes widened. "Nicky too?"

Bertram laughed heartily. "God, no." He wiped a tear from the corner of his eye. "He loves women. He's got a mistress in London. Probably more than just the one."

"I don't doubt that. And he's looking for a wife. Too bad. He *is* rather handsome." Percival's smile darkened. "Like his brother was."

"Like his cousin, as well," Bertram added with a smirk and a bow.

Amusement returned to Percival's eyes.

"And," Bertram continued, "I would love to go to the continent with you and watch sun-browned fishermen and farmers perform physical labors shirtless and carefree. However, I fear my uncle will not be long for this world. I must remain close at hand in case Nicky needs me."

"I understand. I wasn't planning on leaving until...well, you know, after." A sullenness dulled Percival's expression. "For now, I'm home at Wood Hall." He brightened. "Think about it, though?"

"The continent? I would love to go. I've never been."

"Good." Percival gripped Bertram's arm, the touch rousing his cock once again. "Write me when you have time."

"I will." Bertram's heart skipped a beat at the notion of walking barefoot on a beach with his best friend, their hands brushing against each other, finally grasping, a knowing glance precipitating their return to their hotel to further explore their intimacy—

Well, he was allowed his fantasies, and no one would know Percival Wood, the Marquess of Norrington, featured in said fantasies.

Still, he had to stop the fantasy at that moment. Once again he availed himself of his hat.

"Apologies," he said, "I'm expected by my Uncle Robert. I am hoping the earl can impart some engaging stories of my father."

Percival grasped both his hands. "He will, Bertie. I'm sure of it."

The handsome marquess nodded his good day, then turned and strode to his carriage, cutting a fine figure from the backside.

Wood Hall, Hertfordshire

BERTIE'S HANDSOME VISAGE hovered above, lips parted. His tongue flicked along the seam of his smile as he drew closer, his breath mingling with Percy's just before the warm wetness of their mouths merged, their tongues seeking and finding satiation...

Percival jolted awake, the chill of sweat and the stiffness of his cock clear indicators of his eager excitement.

For a kiss.

From a friend.

And it had only been a dream.

He angled his arms over his head, raising his hips and stretching his body against the mattress. Temptation bedeviled him, but he refused to touch himself until he could make sense of his emotions.

Bertram was his dearest friend, probably his only friend. The viscount's letters had kept him thriving and alive throughout his sequestration at Oxford. His pirate adventure stories were so utterly delightful, reminding Percival of his childhood, of a time of creativity, of exuberance, of innocence.

A time before Jack.

Percival squeezed his eyes shut, banking back tears. Bertram's letters had been a balm to his soul, a refuge for his mind. He had eagerly and impatiently awaited each missive.

But were Bertram's stories inciting something else inside? Something he had never known and yet craved?

Like kissing?

Yet Paolo the Pirate Hunter and his friend Barnaby had never kissed—would never kiss. That would be simply silly. They were comrades in arms, focused on quashing evil.

An evil like Jack.

Perhaps with kissing.

Percival stared at the canopy over his bed, the greens of the brocaded fabric discerned only as gray against the gray of night. Avoiding his lamenting cock, he pressed his hand against his heart, the thudding within slowing with each deliberate breath.

The thudding because he had been thinking about kissing.

Percival loved kissing, adored kisses, but he'd rarely received them. He'd always had to beg for kisses from Jack, who used the small act as a bartering chip for some depravity.

Did Bertram enjoy kissing?

Percival sighed. He'd love to find out. Perhaps he would on the continent?

He could only hope. But hope was all he had left, wasn't it?

Percival's life and studies at Oxford had tethered him to the hope that his future held promise, that one day he would be able to explore on his own again, beyond the confines of Jack's world. While studying classics, he had become fascinated with the Etruscans, a race seemingly hidden from history because of the later dominance of Rome.

Much like Percival had been hidden because of Jack.

A tear slid down his temple.

No more hiding, no more being hidden.

He wiped his eyes with the sleeve of his nightshirt. No, he would not shed tears for what he had lost. It was time to explore what could be.

And, possibly, what could be was a kiss from his beloved friend while they explored the continent.

A smile stretched his lips. Well, he could dream, anyway.

* * * * *

Ravensburgh Cottage, Hertfordshire

STANDING AT THE FOOT of his bed, hands tucked in the pockets of his dressing gown, Bertram stared into the dark of his bedroom, a cacophony of emotions coursing through him.

His uncle, his only connection to his Atherley past, was dying.

Yet his future held the promise of an amazing journey.

And his infatuation for Percival was stronger than he'd realized, now that he'd seen the young marquess in the flesh for the first time in almost three years.

Bollocks.

He should be mourning, but he was simply too excited for the possibilities of what lay ahead.

The half-moon, now unsheathed by passing clouds, poured what light it could muster on his uncertain soul. Near the window, on his writing desk, the flame of the oil lamp flickered, illuminating the golden brandy in his crystal goblet and the letter he had not quite finished writing.

To Percival.

He went to the desk, fingers skittering over the polished mahogany before he picked up the letter. The missive continued the adventures of Paolo the Pirate Hunter and his First Mate Barnaby. They had landed at a beach, pistols drawn, and were slogging through the clear blue water tracking the evil pirates who had stolen the gold from a Spanish galleon.

Bertram smiled. He had included a description of Paolo's linen shirt, wet from the spray of breaking waves, clinging to his lithe but muscled torso. He'd contemplated writing Paolo as shirtless, but the notion seemed too ridiculous while one was actively on the hunt. He also did not include how Barnaby dared not stare too much from fear of revealing his attraction. Barnaby merely glanced at his captain when orders were spoken.

Off page, poor Barnaby was bedeviled by desire for his captain and on edge during most of their voyages. He attended

Paolo in his cabin, watching him shave, dress, bathe. He was the true hero, repressing his lust—no, his *love*, for his captain.

All the while Paolo flattered and amused Barnaby, praising him for his cleverness, thanking him for his friendship.

There were many pages buried secretly away in Bertram's desk that delved into Barnaby's lustfulness, how he sought solace with his hand wrapped around his cock, tossing himself to erotic oblivion as he imagined sliding his tongue along the athletic form of his captain.

Bertram's erection pressed against the buttons of his fly. He stared at his glass of brandy, then drained the contents. He needed a better diversion than drink. He really needed a frig.

With only the moon as his witness, he unbuttoned his fly and grabbed his cock.

Had he really just agreed to go to the continent with Percival?

He squeezed his erection, hoping to combat the reckless desire pulsing through his groin, only succeeding in bringing tears to smart his eyes.

Concupiscence took over and he gave in, sliding his fist along the shaft, images of Percival's sultry smile and inviting mouth bombarding his fantasies, the marquess's tongue trailing wetness across his lips to taunt him even more. Bertram arced his spine, tucking his chin, shutting his eyes against the agonizing fantasy. Percival wasn't his. He shouldn't want him, shouldn't be frigging himself while dreaming about him.

Bertram's mind relented as his body released its passion in a sticky mess on his hand. He grabbed his handkerchief and cleaned himself while his lungs pulled in a draught of air to calm his throbbing heart.

How long he'd be able to keep his hands off the handsome marquess, he had no idea.

But he'd have to; he was cocksure of it.

Because Percy was not a brave pirate hunter. No. Rather he was a broken mariner flailing in a sea of terrifying memories.

CHAPTER THREE

*A sextant and a spyglass tell a captain only so much. Who can
really know what lies ahead for a journey on the open sea?*
— *The Adventures of Paolo the Pirate Hunter*

St. Albans, Hertfordshire

Bertram paced outside the decaying Gothic structure that was
the heart of the St. Albans estate. Mason had said he would alert
"his lordship" when the earl had awakened and was ready to see
him. Of course Mason had suggested tea. Bertram had declined.
Tea in a sitting room while the earl lay dying not far away seemed
macabre.

He left the gravel drive and walked until he found a rock upon
which to sit and gaze numbly in the distance. Being out of doors in
the spring air was calming somewhat, and offered more visual and
auditory distractions to the beleaguered mind. Birds, a light
breeze—

"Bertie!"

Bertram stood and turned to the familiar voice calling behind him. A man about his age, with the same color hair. Atherley brown. *My God.* "Nicky."

He stood as Nicholas approached. They stared at each other momentarily, seemingly both equally astonished, then fell together in a hearty hug, emotions shaking their embrace.

Nicholas drew back, still gripping Bertram's shoulders, his gaze darting back and forth, lips curling upward. "It's been a while."

"Seven years, Nicky. It's been seven years since I've seen you."

"You've kept track."

"Well," Bertram sighed, "rather I've had some time to think of the past, our past, in the last few days."

Nicholas sobered. "I, as well." He blinked, revealing a twinkle in his rich, chocolate-brown eyes. Another common feature of the Atherley men. "Thank you for your correspondence over the years."

"With your traipsing over half the globe, it was often difficult to find your whereabouts."

"But you did, and I appreciate it and thank you heartily. Yours were some of the only letters I knew I could read."

Bertram had never bothered writing about family troubles. Instead he had filled the letters with stories about village life, his efforts in his garden, and sometimes politics.

Nicholas released his hold on Bertram's shoulders, looking askance. "Cousin Bertie. You're all the family I have left. I mean after…"

"There's my mother, as well."

Nicholas grinned. "How is my aunt Selina?"

"She currently has a mania for growing cabbages."

"Cabbages?"

"And carrots, and radishes, and herbs, and all sorts of things one might grow and eat. Behind the cottage we now have a glasshouse filled with lemon, orange, and lime trees."

The grin widened. "I'm working with a doctor who has a garden where he grows his own food. He is a follower of vegetarianism."

"Don't tell my mother that! That will be her next fascination and I'll never have roast beef again."

Nicholas laughed.

"So you've finished your medical studies? You're a doctor now?"

"Yes. I finished at Edinburgh Medical School this past winter. Dreariest winter of my life." Nicholas shook his head. "I apologize, Bertie, I should have written or called on you since my return."

"The cottage is on the same estate as all your bad memories." Bertram waved toward the dilapidated manse. "I understand, Nicky, really I do. I should have been the one to visit you in London."

"But you don't like London, do you?"

"I don't know anyone there." Bertram shrugged. "Besides, out here in pastoral Arcadia it's too easy to not deviate from the path of one's usual life."

Nicholas raised a brow over a scrutinizing eye. "There are a lot of writers in London."

"I'd need introductions."

"And I can get them for you."

Bertram sighed in defeat. "You seem determined to get me out of my countrified ways. But I would probably worry too much about Mama being alone."

"She has her cabbages."

Bertram laughed, the joyous emotion rippling through him, liberating a riot of emotions. He met Nicholas's mirth-filled gaze, and both men descended into uncontrollable guffaws.

"I've missed you," Bertram said. "I've missed those moments when you and I—and Percy—could feel so free."

"I agree." Nicholas wiped an eye with his sleeve. "He's back, you know. Percy is home at Wood Hall because of my father's condition."

"I know."

That brightened Nicholas a bit. "Have you seen him, then?"

"Briefly. I am quite affected by how he is handling the situation. A lesser man would not have come. He is quite strong."

"His demons have been dispatched."

Bertram nodded glumly. "Physically, yes. But he still lives with their ghosts, of that I am certain."

Nicholas remained silent.

"How is my Uncle Robert?" Bertram asked.

"Mason told me to fetch you. Papa is awake now."

Bertram smiled. *Papa*. Nicholas had not called his father *Papa* since he was a boy.

Perhaps the demons from one's past could truly, eventually, be exorcised.

Wood Hall, Hertfordshire

"The continent? Now?"

Percival recoiled at Father's tone, laced with incredulity. The duke's pacing across the Persian rug in his study threatened to render the ancient textile threadbare.

"Your mother mentioned something about embarking on a Grand Tour," Father muttered.

"Really just Italy and the Mediterranean coast. I want a bit of culture and sunshine. Mother thinks it's a fine idea." Percival shifted on his feet as he stood his ground near the hearth.

"Norrington," Father began as he stopped in front of him, "the Season is well underway. After this blasted business with St. Albans is finished, we should be in London."

Percival stared at Father, hoping the daggers he was throwing with his glare stung. "This blasted business? You mean once Papa Robert has died?"

Father winced. "I hate that you called him that."

"Present tense, Your Grace. *Call* him. The man is still alive."

"I know. I know," Father said with a sigh and a slump of his shoulders. "But I will never forgive him for letting Jack—" He stopped, his lips pressed into a thin line.

Percival chilled. Did Father know about the true nature of his relationship with Jack? "Letting Jack do what?"

The stunned expression and subsequent pallor revealed Father knew far more than he had ever let on. He sucked air through his teeth. "Do such horrible things to you."

"You mean taking me to his bed?"

The pallor reddened. Father glanced away. "No. That is…insignificant to the abuse you suffered."

"You knew."

"Of course I knew. I saw the bruises. I had you sent away to Oxford—"

"No. I mean, you knew we were lovers. You've never admitted that."

Father straightened and took a step back. "There was never any need to call attention to the matter. What malevolence had been brought upon you was far more consequential."

"But you think Papa Robert—pardon me, the Earl of St. Albans, knew about Jack's abuse while it happened?"

"He had to."

"The earl confessed he had no idea Jack hurt me."

"How could he not know what was going on under his own roof?" Father bellowed.

"Because it usually did not take place under his own roof, but in the lairs of Jack's friends."

A grimace. "But he knew his own son was a pederast. Jack was so much older than you."

"And now you know your own son is a catamite."

The color drained from Father's face. A juddering exhalation revealed he was trying to contain some emotion. He gripped Percival's shoulders. "Norrington." Another exhalation. "Percy, son, yes, I knew about you and Jack, that you were more than mere drinking and gambling companions. One of the best kept secrets in this day and age is that there are indeed others like you. A lot more than you might think."

Dumbstruck, Percival's jaw dropped.

Father gestured that they should sit. His legs about to give out, Percival quickly sunk into the generous velvet sofa. Father pulled up a side chair alongside and sat.

"I knew about Jack's intentions." Father scowled. "I told him I wanted your relationship to be respectable until you were older."

"If you mean we only drank and gambled until I was older, that was the case."

"I know. I made sure of it."

"What do you mean?"

"As long as he kept his hands off you, I paid some of his gambling debts."

"You were part of this?"

"I was protecting you."

"But then you stopped. Why did you stop?"

"You were older and seemed to be in love with him."

Percival stared at the carpet. "I think I might have been for a spell. Or whatever a lad of seventeen thinks is love."

"So I let you have your affair. Best to get it out of your system while you're young."

Out of his system? Father really did not understand. Desire for men was part of him, not a passing preoccupation.

"What I did not know," Father continued, his voice gravelly, "was that he was cruel to you. Please believe me when I say this. You hid it well."

Avoiding and lying to Father were rather easy.

"I did not know until…" Father cleared his throat, "that day."

"When Mama Louisa was killed."

Father shuddered. "She was a wonderful, patient woman." He closed his eyes a moment and breathed deeply before wiping away a tear. "You needed to be removed from Jack's drunken violence and profligate ways. And you needed protection. Rage fueled by jealousy can be deadly. That is why I had you under surveillance at Oxford."

"Your spies were quite clever. But I knew who they were."

Father chuckled. "Luckily, Jack obliterated himself with drink after that. I admit I had prayed Jack would find an early grave. For your sake." He looked at the ceiling. "May God understand when it is my time to go."

Percival remained silent.

"This escape abroad will give you distance, so I will agree to it." Father leaned forward, his elbows on his knees. "But Percy, once you return you must focus on your duties. You've grown. It is time to put foolish games away."

"Since you already know the true nature of my relationship with Jack, please know that such feelings are not foolish games. I am what I am."

Father cleared his throat. "As the Marquess of Norrington you have a duty to the Amesbury title. You must not forget that."

"As your only son and heir, I am exceedingly aware of my place, and have been all my life."

"Norrington, you must marry and produce an heir. I had hoped you would accept invitations to events this Season. To have a debut, so to speak. To publicly proclaim you have put the whole situation with Jack behind you and show you have emerged unscathed."

Emerged, like a butterfly from a cocoon. "I'm not certain I'm strong enough for that at the moment. People will whisper. And I don't know how I will react if I happen to see one of Jack's old friends. Not now, at least. I need some time. I'm only twenty-one.

I'll still be marriageable next year at twenty-two." Or even a dozen years hence. Or more.

"Yes, I suppose you're right. It is more important for you to take the opportunity to mend." Father rose and went to his desk. He removed his cigar box, pulling two out. "Do you smoke cigars?" He let out a dull chuckle. "I don't even know if you smoke cigars."

"I don't. Perhaps Ravensburgh will teach me when we're on the continent."

Father's eyebrows arched as he lit and puffed on his cigar. "Ravensburgh? The Viscount Ravensburgh?"

"I've invited him on my journey, and he has agreed."

"Another man? There might be gossip this close to Jack's death."

"Father, Bertie is my closest friend. My childhood friend. There is nothing perverse about our relationship." *Except for last night's surprisingly erotic dream.* "I guarantee there will be no gossip. Besides, the Earl of St. Albans is his uncle. It would not seem so unusual for the two of us needing to escape after such a tragedy."

"I suppose Ravensburgh's presence as your companion will make a show that there is no continued ill-will toward the Atherley family."

Percival breathed out relief. "Plus, as our neighbors, and with Nicholas in line for the earldom, these connections will be important."

"Oxford has made you wise," Father said with a chuckle. "And I hope the continent will refresh you." He puffed on his cigar, then stared at the ash forming at the end. "I'll give you letters of introduction for my contacts in Paris."

"I'm not going to Paris, Father."

The duke's gray-blue eyes widened. "Why on earth not? You've never been."

"And one day I *will* go, Father. Just not now."

"Percy, your chances of meeting aristocratic families outside of Paris are slim. We just talked about your duty to marry."

Something he did not want to think about. Ever. Definitely not at that moment. "Paris is too close to London. Too close to the past."

"Hmm," Father grunted through a haze of smoke. "Jack's friends frequent Paris?"

"They have been known to visit." Percival exhaled in frustration. "Another time, Father. I'll meet your contacts another time."

"Of course." A touch of empathy had filtered into Father's tone. He sucked on his cigar. "So where is it you want to go?"

"Professor Bellamy has recommended a stay in Umbria to see the landscape and imagine the ancient Etruscans. I thought perhaps to go along the Mediterranean coast after that, where there's sun and beaches, and not all this rain."

Father's rare chuckle and smile were genuine. "All right, you deserve a diverting holiday."

He did.

"Will you be going to the southern coast of France? Perhaps to Nice?"

His plans were still in a nascent stage. "I suppose I could. I've heard it's a lovely town."

Father chomped his cigar as he rummaged around in his desk. "I have names of some English expatriates living in Nice. Old friends of mine. I'll write letters of introduction. Perhaps they can introduce you to suitable young women." He chuckled. "That would be well worth your journey."

Not bloody likely. Percival smiled. "Thank you, Father. I'll be happy to meet your friends." He would do what he had to do for the Amesbury title. Besides, doing his duty would not seem so horrid with Bertram at his side.

* * * * *

St. Albans, Hertfordshire

"GEORGE? Is that you?"

Bertram chilled despite the humid warmth of the St. Albans morning room. George—Bertram's father—had died over twenty years ago.

The earl stared at him with glassy eyes as he lay on his cot. Clearly, the time was very soon.

"No, Uncle Robert. It is me, Bertram. George's son."

A gentle knock on the door precipitated Nicholas's entrance. He nodded his greeting at Bertram, then pulled up a chair to sit next to him. Nicholas took the earl's hand. "Papa, I'm here."

"Nicky. Do you not think Bertram looks like George?"

Nicholas thinned his lips and simply nodded. Nicholas had been four or five when his Uncle George had died. He wouldn't remember what he looked like.

George had been about thirty-four at his death, but he'd left England for the Crimea at least a year before that. And now Bertram was twenty-eight...

The dying earl was probably right, then. At that moment, Bertram most likely looked quite a bit like his father had the last time the earl had seen him.

And now Uncle Robert was about to meet his younger brother in heaven.

"Well, Bertram, I must say you are as handsome as George." Uncle Robert smiled at Nicholas. "George was the handsome one in the family."

Bertram held his amusement in check. Of them all, Nicholas was by far the most handsome.

"I'm proud of my brother," continued Uncle Robert. "I hope you marry a beauty like your mother and have many children to continue George's well-deserved titles."

"When I am ready, Uncle Robert." Bertram had no intention of marriage and children. But now was not the time to make such bold proclamations.

Father had never used his titles—he'd never had the opportunity. The titles Viscount Ravensburgh and Baron Hexton had been granted posthumously by Queen Victoria for his service in Crimea. There really was no need to continue the lineage for such recent honors. A historical peerage was far more important. Such as the earldom of St. Albans, which went back centuries.

"Good, good." Uncle Robert smiled weakly. "You are a fine young man, Bertram. George would be proud of you. Make him more proud."

Tears burned Bertram's eyes. "Yes, Uncle. Thank you."

"I'm tired. I think I should rest now."

Bertram's vision blurred. There was not much time left. He should say what he needed to say. Even if Uncle Robert was no longer listening.

"Uncle, thank you for indulging me when I was young. For permitting me and my companions to play on the grounds of the estate." Away from his own home with its solemn responsibilities. "For guiding me on how to be a proper peer. For helping Mama when she was left widowed."

"Louisa was such a strength to her, then."

Bertram released his control over his emotions. No point in pretending he was not crying. "I know."

"I cannot wait to see my wife again. I hope I will see her again."

Nicholas paled. "Of course you will see Mama. She will insist on escorting you through the gates of heaven."

The earl closed his eyes. Moments later quiet, rhythmic snores escaped his open mouth.

Nicholas placed his hand on Bertram's knee. "I'll stay a little longer. He just needs his rest. It's not quite time." As a doctor, Nicholas would know such things.

"Thank you, Nicky."

"Stay here, Bertie. Mason can prepare tea."

"I think I need a walk."

"Yes, all right. I'll find you presently."

Once out of the house, Bertram roamed, aimlessly, probably in circles. It did not matter.

He'd barely cried when Papa had died. He hadn't quite understood that Papa was never coming back. Papa had been gone for so long that Bertram had started to forget him. He'd been simply too young to comprehend memories and death.

Guilt and regret broke out as sweat upon his brow, tears on his cheeks. He leaned against a boulder to support his now shaking body. Uncle Robert had been more father to him than Papa had ever had time to be. Yet he loved Papa more than he loved Uncle Robert.

To a child, a father had no sins. But as the child grew, a father's faults were revealed. Bertram had one father as a child and another as an adult. Had he judged Uncle Robert too harshly?

He gazed out over the landscape, weedy and overgrown. He and Nicholas and Percival had spent so much time there. Percival had told them fantastical stories of fairies who lived in the trunks of trees and beneath boulders. As he grew, the stories became more outlandish, his gestures unbridled as he expounded upon the details of non-existent pirate ships, creating a shoreline where there was nothing but unmown grass, inventing plots that kept Bertram and Nicholas intrigued until the end.

Not one of the three had ever had a close relationship with their respective fathers.

And now all of them were about to have their lives changed irrevocably. Nicholas because he stood to inherit an estate and title. Percy because he was now released from a prison of fear.

And Bertram because he was now free to hope for something beyond friendship with Percival.

"Bertie?" Nicholas approached, his face tear-stained.

"How is he?"

"Sleeping. Mason is with him." Nicholas pulled out a handkerchief from an inside jacket pocket and dabbed his eyes. The letter *R* was embroidered in one corner of the linen square.

Ramsay. Nicholas's mother's surname. More evidence of the strain between father and son.

"Come sit." Bertram patted a spot of rock.

Nicholas sat. "I do believe this was one of the boulders under which the fairies lived."

Bertram chuckled. "Yes, I think so."

"I'm not prepared for this, Bertie. I thought I would have time to create a name for myself, create a life for myself. Papa's not so very old." Nicholas glanced his way. "I think this is how you must have felt as a child."

"Overwhelmed?"

"Precisely." Nicholas let out a heavy sigh. "I'm not certain a will has been drawn up for this sudden turn of events. I told Papa I was never meant to be the Earl of St. Albans. I'm not even interested in becoming earl." Another glance. "I told him you would be a far better earl than I could ever be."

What? "Me?"

"Yes. You've taken to your father's viscountcy with grace and dignity. The Atherley name needs a man such as you to restore our good standing."

Oh, no. He was *not* going to be that man. "I am flattered you think so. If the honor befalls me, Nicky, I will certainly accept my duty," he said quietly. "But right now I am in love and I would like to immerse myself in that luscious feeling for a moment. I really don't want the headache of this estate. I'm sure you understand."

"You're in love? How marvelous."

"It is, rather. And I think you underestimate yourself. You would make a fine earl." He tapped Nicholas on the knee as he stood. "I will leave you alone to contemplate your future. And I will contemplate the possibilities of my own."

CHAPTER FOUR

"Raise a glass to those intrepid adventurers who have come before.
For it is because of them that we know the way."
— *The Adventures of Paolo the Pirate Hunter*

Wood Hall, Hertfordshire

It happened last night, a rainy night not unlike any other during a late English spring. But the note from Nicholas delivered by messenger that morning brought with it the freezing chill of winter.

The Earl of St. Albans—Papa Robert—had died, the official cause given as infection due to a gunshot wound. He had passed peacefully in his sleep. There would be no funeral.

Percival rolled onto his back on the daybed in his sitting room, the note now crumpled in his hand, staring at the painted scene on the ceiling. The lines and colors blurred as tears slid down his temples to his ears. Papa Robert was dead. All scandal—

and any further monetary outlay by the thoroughly indebted estate—would be avoided by not having a funeral.

He squelched a sob.

The past was dead. Long live the future.

After a fortifying exhalation, Percival pulled out his handkerchief and wiped his tears. The painting on the ceiling came into focus. Britannia had been recrowned and Neptune had restored the command of the seas to her. An allegory that seemed like it should be pertinent to his current state of emotions, but somehow only uncovered the amusements of his boyhood. He never did care for the uncovered breasts of the nereids, but instead targeted his intentions on the bare chests of the attending sea-gods.

A knock on his door sent him sitting straight up.

"Norrington? Are you in there?" Mother's voice held apprehension.

He dabbed any residual traces of sorrow with his handkerchief. "Yes, Mother. Please come in."

She went to him the moment she entered, her face crinkled with concern, her blue eyes glassy from impending tears. "Oh, Norrington. I was afraid you would be mired in despair." She sat at his side and wrapped an arm around his shoulders.

He leaned against her, the uncharacteristic sympathy comforting. "I'm still in shock, I think. I need some time to comprehend all that has happened."

"St. Albans was kind to you."

"He was." *And more of a father than Father ever was.*

"I agree it will take time to comprehend your loss. Your voyage will do you good. A great deal of adventures await you on the continent." She sighed. "I only wish you were finding your entertainment in a ballroom this Season."

Oh, no. Not the talk of marriage again. "Mother, I do not want to have to think about marriage." He pulled out of her embrace. "Especially not right now. But not at my age either. Why, I haven't even finished university yet."

"Ah, yes," she said almost absentmindedly. "You really should complete your studies at Oxford. You are so very close to finishing. I'll inform the duke."

"But why is he so adamant I marry?"

Mother sighed again, this time a little more loudly. "If you marry and settle down, society will see that the relationship with Jack was merely a youthful indiscretion."

"Youthful indiscretion? Is that your phrase for it? For describing what I am?"

She flushed. "Norrington," she began softly, "your father and I do not care if you take up with men, although the duke will never admit that to you."

The revelation was rather surprising.

"All we ask is that you be discreet about it. Very discreet. The Amesbury name cannot afford another scandal. Let Jack's scandal be associated with the St. Albans name while you create some distance."

"I see. So you want me to bind myself to some unsuspecting girl for the rest of my life because of what society thinks?"

Mother stared icily. "Continence and propriety are the duties of the aristocracy in this country. We gave you your freedom in your boyhood. But your freedom only extends so far, Norrington. This is true for all sons of dukes."

"Yes, Mother."

"Your duty also includes marrying a respectable girl and producing an heir. And while it is true men may wait until their dotage to produce children, I think the duke is concerned that if he does not see you married and become a father in his lifetime, you will shirk your duties. I tried to convince him you have plenty of time. He's only fifty-four. But St. Albans' unexpected death has only instilled anxiety regarding his own mortality."

Mother rose and sauntered to his wardrobe. She opened the doors and began perusing his clothes.

"We all have our secrets, Norrington," she said. "How we keep them is important."

Secrets? Did Mother and Father harbor secrets? "Yes, Mother."

She turned and smiled at him. "But Norrington…Percival, please take your time with this adventure. Spend time with your boyhood friend reminiscing. Take in the sights and sounds and smells of Italy and France. This is part of the freedom you do have. The freedom of money and position and being a handsome young man. Take advantage of this."

"Thank you, Mother. I would like to enjoy my holiday without stress."

"And you will. I'll oversee your packing with Armand so you needn't even worry about that." She tapped a finger against her lips in thoughtfulness. "Armand is a most excellent valet. He'll be a valuable asset to your time on the continent. He was born in France, did you know?" The pitch of her voice increased just a little. "And he knows about you…about your past. I think he understands it, as well. He'll take very good care of you." She smiled. "He always has, hasn't he?"

"Yes, Mother." Armand had been with him since he was a boy, remained stalwart while he was with Jack, stayed by his side all through Oxford.

"He'll handle the details of your itinerary, as well. I don't want you to worry about a thing, Norrington."

Good. He could spend his time dreaming of Bertie.

Ravensburgh Cottage, Hertfordshire

Bertram adjusted the pillow behind his back in the library window seat to get a better view of the moon. Phoebus's orb glowed behind a shroud of wispy clouds, while a gentle breeze tugged at the celestial mist in an attempt to uncover the beauty for all the world to see.

The day had been difficult emotionally. Not as much as Friday, when he'd received a missive from Nicholas that the Earl of St. Albans had died. Poor Nicholas, fatherless as himself, the journey of life ahead completely rudderless.

Except he and Nicholas had always been able to navigate without the usual tools of guidance.

Mason had followed up with a letter detailing the events to come. The reading of the will would take place in June. Bertram should not expect to receive anything, as there was not much left to the estate but debt and debilitation. As such, he need not be present.

That was all very fine for Bertram.

He'd wiped a tear then dashed off a note to Percival. He would be ready to leave for the continent at a moment's notice. Mourning with the marquess while riding continental railways would be preferable to any other traditional custom.

He sipped his brandy, savoring the burn down his throat, as the almost full moon won its battle with the clouds.

The last moments with Uncle Robert had been unexpectedly joyous, given the familial past. Uncle Robert had been forthcoming with stories of Mama and Papa. Recounting memories had seemed to revive him somewhat.

"George loved your mother. I remember when he first met Selina, the light in his eyes. Tremendous. They waited to have children, you know. They simply loved spending time together. Just the two of them, alone."

"Why did my father join the army?"

"I suppose that's my fault. Well, I mean, I'm the eldest. I inherited the title. George wanted to serve Queen and country. He couldn't do it in Parliament, so he chose the army." Uncle Robert had coughed at that moment, an unnatural cough. "He would have been a far better Parliamentarian than I ever was."

There had been a long silence after that. Long enough that Bertram began to worry if he should call for Mason. But after a sputtering episode of hacking, the earl livened.

"A tragedy. A blasted tragedy," he muttered.

"What is, Uncle?"

"My life. I regret almost all of it." More hacking. "Except Nicholas. I don't regret him." Uncle Robert had grasped Bertram's hand with a grip that belied his wounded state. "Don't have regrets, my boy. I would tell you to never get old, but I hope you live a long life for your father's sake. Just don't live a life with regrets."

Bertram had left soon after, somewhat overwhelmed by the whole experience.

The memory spiked new tears in his eyes. No regrets. That's why he'd accepted Percival's invitation to travel. He wanted the chance to deepen their friendship.

A light knock preceded the opening of the library door. "Bertram?"

The concern in Mama's voice quickly turned to a giggling admonishment as Winifred, her devoted Blenheim spaniel, came charging into the library. Bertram set down his brandy as Winifred lengthened her body until her paws rested on the top of the window seat. She let out a pleading whimper. Bertram picked her up, gave her a nuzzle, then held her wriggling form aloft.

"My diminutive miniature Winifred." He kissed her snout, but pulled back when she tried to lick him. "My dimi mini Wini."

"Sounds like a Latin declension," Mama said, still standing by the open door. "Why are you sitting in the dark, Bertram?"

"Mama, come." He gathered Winifred into his lap and patted the seat next to him. "Pour yourself a brandy."

By the light of a dim oil lamp on the library table, she availed herself of the decanter of brandy. She approached. "Is the death of your Uncle Robert so affecting you must sit in the dark?"

"No." He chuckled. "The moon is beautiful tonight."

"Ah." She hid a smile behind her snifter.

"You're amused."

Mama sat opposite and gazed out beyond the leaded glass panes. "The moon is beautiful every night, but you have only just noticed." She took a bold draught of brandy. "You never told me about your last moments with your uncle."

"I asked about Papa, for him to tell me some stories. He said you and Papa were very much in love."

She snorted a laugh. "We were. We are. I am. He is simply no longer present at my side." This time her sip of brandy was more thoughtful.

"Uncle Robert had changed since the last time I saw him." Bertram shook his head. "I don't just mean physically. That *was* rather a shock. But in his heart."

"More philosophic."

How astute Mama was. "Yes."

"He's been becoming that way since Louisa died. I think the horror of it all made him realize how much she meant to him."

"Unlike you and Papa."

A crease formed between Mama's brows. "How do you mean?"

"You knew how much Papa meant to you long before he died."

"I did."

"How did you know?"

Her lips spread into a faraway smile. "I think it was when he began calling, but I was always preoccupied with my sister and her beaux. And yet, he remained undeterred."

"Simple persistence?"

She laughed softly. "No. Patience is the more apt description." She turned her head to look at the moon, the glow highlighting the pearl necklace she wore. A gift from Papa. "George was patient."

And there she sat, the Viscountess of Ravensburgh, a woman in her prime of life, patiently waiting to be with her husband again. Waiting while Bertram figured out his own damn life.

She revived and met his gaze. "There is something else, Bertram. Tell me."

"I saw Nicholas." He paused.

Mama waited, but when Bertram did not have the courage to speak, she proceeded. "He's become a fine man indeed. His prospects for working in his new profession in London look good. I spoke with him yesterday."

Bertram took a sip of brandy. "And Percy."

She gaped. "Young Percival? The Marquess of Norrington?"

"The very same."

"Oh, my." She paled, then stared at the dregs clinging to her crystal snifter. "That poor boy."

She knew. Mama knew.

"He's invited me to the continent. A Grand Tour of sorts."

She brightened. "Oh, how lovely. You must go, of course." She looked into her glass. "We'll manage whatever costs."

"Percy has offered to stand the cost, Mama," he said gently.

She raised her head abruptly, her gape fleeting. "How very generous. You never had your Grand Tour, and if the marquess wants to sponsor your joining him, I take no issue with that."

"I'm glad you approve."

"Naturally, I approve. You and Percival were always such a pair. I think you will be good for him."

He certainly hoped so, but not in any way Mama was probably imagining.

"Our families have been cordial over the years, Bertram," Mama continued. "I know there was a scandal involving young Percival and I know St. Albans was somehow involved—"

"Mama, rest assured the earl did nothing to hurt Percy."

"I know what my brother-in-law was capable of," she said in a clipped tone. "One day the truth will come out about his treatment of poor Louisa, and why Nicholas escaped to faraway lands."

One day. Perhaps. That would have to be up to Nicky. It was his scandal now.

"Your father was an upstanding man, but even his reputation could not save the Atherley family. Louisa did her best to keep society from giving us the cut." Mama exhaled heavily. "We all knew what Jack was."

"What Jack was?" Bertram blurted. "Inverted?"

Winifred squirmed in his lap as if sensing his indignation. He kept his anger in check.

Mama narrowed her eyes, now clouded with curiosity and suspicion. "I don't know that word."

"Pardon me, Mama. I should not use such language with you."

"Bertram, tell me what that means."

He drew in a long breath. "A sexually inverted man is a man who lies with other men."

Mama sucked in her lower lip and shook her head. "Yes, the family did know that about Jack. But that's not what I meant. I meant he was a villain. An abusive villain." She met Bertram's gaze. "What two people may do behind closed doors is none of my concern as long as no one is hurt. Poor Percy was hurt."

Her eyes widened as she stared at him. He drew in a breath, waiting.

She looked away, her lower lip between her teeth. As if she were preventing herself from speaking aloud.

Bertram slowly exhaled. Realization must have suddenly dawned on her. He'd never mentioned any women, and she'd never asked. Since leaving Cambridge, he'd visited friends from that time in his life, but had never mentioned their sisters. He'd attended village assemblies, but had never formed an attachment to any of his dance partners. Mama did know, however, that he'd been corresponding with Percival.

"Like I said, Bertram, I think your presence will soothe Percy's battered soul."

Winifred shifted once again, this time with determination. Bertram let her go, and she padded over to Mama's lap where she curled up.

"Your father's watch."

Mama's voice was wistful. Bertram glanced down at his disheveled jacket, the watch attached to his waistcoat now revealed.

He unfastened the chain from the buttonhole and handed the watch to her.

She studied it, turning it over in her palm reverently, the gold glinting in the moonlight. "I haven't seen this in a while." She opened the engraved cover revealing her portrait Papa had carried with him at all times. Melancholia clouded her face. "I was a beautiful creature in my youth."

"You are still beautiful, Mama."

A smile brightened her face. She handed the watch back to him. "Thank you, Bertram."

"Will you be all right without me, Mama? When I'm on the continent? When I'm with Percy? I'll make sure to supply you with our itinerary and the addresses of our hotels. Or wherever we'll be staying. I don't actually know yet."

The smile widened, perhaps knowingly. "Oh, pshaw. I have my books and my garden. I'll take walks into the village. And I'll have my friends over for tea more often." One corner of her mouth lifted in an expression bordering on mischievous. As if she were suddenly looking forward to his being gone for a spell.

She coaxed Winifred to the carpet, then rose, a sense of satisfaction seemingly replacing the earlier disquietude. "Well, I am off to bed. Don't stay up too late, Bertram." She bent her face to his, and he kissed her cheek. She placed her glass on the library table and left, Winifred at her heels.

Brandy in hand, Bertram resumed his contemplation of the moon. He was quite lucky to have been born into the less tumultuous side of the family.

~ INTERLUDE ~

The Adventures of Paolo the Pirate Hunter, the Magnificent Adventurer, who, along with his First Mate Barnaby, Protects the Seas from the Evil Pirate Jonas the Marauder

by Bertram Atherley, The Right Honorable 2nd Viscount Ravensburgh

From the white sand shoreline, Paolo gazed out over the endless sea, the horizon mocking him with its infinity.

Beside him his loyal and trusty companion Barnaby Heath remained stoic and still as he also stared with blank expression, likely stunned at their utter defeat.

For they had once again failed to capture the notorious pirate Jonas the Marauder.

"He is a corrupt and depraved opponent, my captain." Barnaby's words were meant to assuage wounded pride for he never condescended to comparative flattery. "The pirate is a most abhorrent villain. As an honorable man, I know you will not stoop to the depths of such wickedness in order to vanquish him."

Paolo shook himself free from his dull inertia. "No. I will not. But I will endeavor to persevere. He must be stopped."

Like an unseen ghost, the villain had too easily slipped away. Chasing down such an apparition would be a daunting task, but a burden that needed to be shouldered.

Interviews with Tortuga's inhabitants had revealed the depths of the pirate's infamy. Ransoms had been extorted, precious heirlooms pillaged, maidens ruined of their innocence, youths pressed into service.

The pirate had escaped unscathed during the chaos of the explosion.

Paolo fought against the ire of yet another defeat. Anger was a hindrance to action.

The weight of Barnaby's hand on his shoulder livened him from his funk. "Captain, I remain at your side." A gentle breeze tousled chestnut strands across his first mate's forehead.

"Onward, then. We have a pirate to catch."

~ * ~ * ~ * ~

CHAPTER FIVE

A tankard of ale and a gambol in a port town—these make for a
satisfied and loyal crew.
— The Adventures of Paolo the Pirate Hunter

London, June 1879

Gray morning light wrapped in steam filtered through the
iron trusses of the roof of Charing Cross station. Passengers and
their well-wishers scurried about on the crowded railway platform.
The acrid smell of burning coal lingered in the air. Bertram had not
traveled in a long time, and never to the continent. Excitement
burbled through him now, and had kept him awake most of the
night.

Further along the platform, Percival and his valet directed
railway porters in the proper handling of his baggage. Bertram
climbed the steps to the first class carriage, his excitement
overtaken by a slight uneasiness.

He had servants, of course, but only enough to maintain the estate left by his father. He lived frugally and did not employ a valet. Although perhaps he should. Percival was impeccably dressed at all times and truly had the aura and appearance of a duke's heir.

Bertram smoothed down his jacket. He wasn't shabby, just not Percival. The lack of a personal manservant meant he was not as flawless as his traveling companion.

Shouts outside the carriage signaled the imminent departure of the train. Bertram took the window seat facing the direction the train would move in. He couldn't abide rail travel in the wrong direction.

Percival entered, then stood in the middle of the car, regarding both benches, finally choosing the one on which Bertram sat, but occupying the opposite end, nearest the door.

"Why sit so far away?"

"I prefer sitting next to the window." Percival smiled briefly. "Rail travel is terribly uncomfortable when one faces the wrong direction."

Bertram chuckled.

"What is so amusing, my lord?" Percival emphasized the honorific with a hint of jocularity.

"It seems you and I both feel the same way."

A blush brightened Percival's cheeks. But a sharp knock on the carriage door startled him, the blush swiftly fading.

Percival's valet opened the door. "Some refreshment for your journey, my lord. And the book bag you requested."

The man hauled up a wicker hamper and a Gladstone bag, his strength belied by his wiry, middle-aged frame. Percival helped drag the luggage further into the carriage, bumping against Bertram's knees.

Evoking a delightful, if brief, thrill.

"I will be in the next compartment, my lord," the valet said with a sort of calm reassurance. "I will see you on the packet ship to Boulogne."

Percival nodded. "Thank you, Armand."

There was a gentle familiarity between the two. Of course, after all of Percival's tribulations, they would naturally have a bond. Armand was probably more like a father to the marquess than was the duke himself.

Percival sat, his thighs straddling the Gladstone bag, his right knee almost touching Bertram. A little shift in his seat, and Bertram was even closer.

"I've packed a great deal to keep us occupied." Percival opened the hinged top of the leather bag and poked around, finally pulling out two new cloth-bound volumes. "For me, I have *Cities and Cemeteries of Etruria* by George Dennis." He gave the embossed title of one of the covers a reverent stroke before placing the books on the bench. "But there are travel guides and language books—"

The train lurched, jostling Percival against him.

Bertram relished the moment. He breathed in the marquess's cologne, subtle and seductive. Percival quickly righted himself. Bertram straightened his waistcoat and jacket, deflecting his disappointment.

Percival brushed the lapels of Bertram's jacket. "So sorry, Bertie. Did I muss you terribly?" He continued his brushing further along to his trousers.

"Oh, no, my lord. Not too terribly so." Bertram tried to keep the huskiness from his voice while unable to tame the stirring in his crotch.

Percival pulled back, biting his lower lip, a touch of shock on his face. He quickly sat back against the upholstered banquette, folding his hands in his lap briefly before toying with one of his Etruscan volumes.

Had the marquess felt something? It was unclear if his current demeanor expressed embarrassment or dismay.

Or arousal.

Bertram bent over the open bag. "I thought I might make a study of Italian. I only brought a study guide and a dictionary, though. Well, beside my notebooks. I plan on revising and expanding the Paolo the Pirate Hunter story."

That enlivened Percival. "How marvelous."

"But what else do you have here? A Baedeker?" Bertram pulled out a red volume. *"The Traveller's Manual of Conversation in Four Languages: English, German, French, Italian.* That should keep me occupied for a bit."

"I regret to say it will have to do for much longer than a bit." Percival sighed. "Our journey will not be like a typical Grand Tour. Any reasonable Englishman would stop along the way. Dinner in Paris. Explore the Mediterranean coast. I just want to get there and be done with it."

Get as far away—and quickly—from the burden of memories.

"Which means we'll be sleeping in rail cars. On the seats." He rubbed the velvet of the upholstery. "It will be nine and a half hours to Paris. Then we will travel directly to Italy." Percival pouted as he glanced out his window. "I fear we will not get much rest until we arrive at Orvieto."

Bertram had no concept of how long the journey might take, but Percival already sounded exhausted.

"Armand assured me that some of the carriages will have seats that pull out and form a sort of crude bed. So we will be able to sleep off and on."

"Sounds like an adventure, Percy. Like camping out."

"I suppose. Perhaps," Percival admitted with an exhalation. "Well, then, I will take my place on the other side of the bench with the Etruscans." He eyed the hamper. "Feel free to avail yourself of refreshment. Armand has exquisite tastes when it comes to snacks and picnic luncheons."

"Thank you, Percy. I will." Bertram was still satisfied from pecking at his breakfast earlier that morning. But now that he was on the moving train and excitement was mellowing, his appetite would revive.

He shifted in his seat and set his gaze out at the swiftly passing landscape, his hands idly stroking the language guide as his mind wandered on the journey ahead. Crossing the English Channel would certainly provide valuable insights for Paolo the Pirate Hunter.

But there would be plenty of train rides ahead. First-class carriages with just him and Percival in an intimate space. Sometimes sleeping.

The prospect of travel had never been so appealing.

PERCIVAL AWOKE, disorientation befuddling his senses for a moment before the sway of the rail car reminded him where he was. Somewhere in Italy. So it must be Thursday.

What time was it? Morning, of course, but when? Very late, most likely. He hadn't felt so relaxed and well-rested in a long time. Tucked away in a corner of the rail car on a fold-out bed next to one's very good friend seemed to give him more of a sense of security than a bulky bodyguard outside his door at Oxford.

He peeked over the blanket to survey the scene beyond. The bedding of Bertram's berth was pulled back revealing empty sheets. A twinge of panic startled Percival, until the viscount's bum came into view, then the rest of him as he unfolded his frame from digging through his luggage.

Percival stifled a gasp. Bertram was wearing only his drawers. He was completely nude on top.

Oh my.

He cut a fine figure, a very fine figure. A sculpture of a Greek athlete come to life except the flesh was a shade of sun-kissed buff and not marble-white. Muscled shoulders and upper arms framed a slender torso. The band of his drawers clung snugly around his narrow waist. His abdomen rippled in muscular waves, the taut pectorals furred with a fine dusting of brown hair.

Percival's cock, already hard just from the simple act of waking up, remained in its excited state, now no longer merely an inevitable physiological reaction, but a call to urgent action.

Good God. Tossing off while spying on one's dear friend—no matter how positively perfect he was—would not be polite. But cocks did not care a whit about civilities.

As stealthily as possible in such close quarters, Percival slid his hand under the hem of his nightshirt to grip his stiff stander. The damn thing would have to be content with that. He wasn't about to make a shameful scene.

Bertram stood before a small mirror hung on the wood paneling examining the stubble along his jawline. He set out his razor, a bowl with his brush, and a towel on the edge of his bed. The viscount was skilled in shaving himself, as he always had done. He'd even said he would be happy to teach Percival for those days when Armand was indisposed, although Percival certainly did not need to shave very often. The ritual—and attending conversation—had taken place yesterday morning, and Percival had thought nothing of it. But this morning, he and his cock were anticipating the show.

What on earth had changed?

That sense of security? Was he more open to possibilities now that possibilities offered peace of mind?

Arm and shoulder muscles tensed and flexed with each scrape of the shaving blade, each practiced movement graceful, mesmerizing to observe. The routine act was now imbued with sensuality. Percival gripped his cock harder.

Bertram cleaned his face with his towel, checking his cheeks in the mirror. He stopped, staring harder into the mirror. Had the blade missed a spot?

"How long have you been watching me, my lord?"

Damn. Found out. His cock retreated.

"Since I awoke and found you missing."

"Did you finally learn how to accomplish the act?"

Percival chuckled. "I think I should not want to perform any activity involving a sharp blade whilst on a moving train."

"We'll have our first lesson, then, in a steady room in Italy."

"I think that would be best."

Bertram climbed onto his side of the bed, propping himself on an elbow next to Percival, his bare torso so close, too close. Percival could simply reach out and touch the fine hair on that athletic chest—

"I've never heard you snore until last night." Bertram's grin was crooked, teasing. "Does that mean you slept well?"

"I did sleep well, thank you. And I do not snore."

"There's a first time for everything." Bertram winked. He left Percival's side and went to his travel wardrobe. "Whenever you're ready, my lord, I'm here to help you dress."

Another task Armand was not available for, given Percival's insistence on such a tight itinerary. Bertram's self-sufficiency once again proved useful.

Percival tugged down his nightshirt. His cock had reduced to a slack state, greatly disappointed. Erotic relief would have to wait. Now it was time to arise and start the day.

He glanced over at Bertram. What a fine day it was proving to be.

"THERE it is."

Bertram slid along the bench in the rail car until he was a little too close to Percival and looked out the window. A dramatic rocky outcropping with buttresses and towers loomed in the distance. A welcome sight to a travel-weary soul.

Orvieto. Finally.

The station was the stop before their final destination and where, presumably, a carriage waited to take them to a villa. Bertram livened up a bit as the train pulled into the station located at the base of the medieval hill-town.

They had been traveling via rail non-stop for three days, at times the train simply plodding along at a drudgingly slow pace. Day revealed landscapes of striking mountainous terrain, or flatlands dotted with farms and ancient stone buildings. Night revealed his infatuation with Percival was becoming more and more difficult to contain, especially when he slept at the marquess's side.

Perhaps the last few days of tedious confinement had been restorative to Percival. Bertram, for his part, had spent the time distracting himself with learning Italian. He was becoming proficient in reading the language, but rarely got chances to hear it spoken other than conductors yelling instructions on railway platforms. Most likely his accent would be atrocious and whatever he said would be incomprehensible.

What he would have preferred to have been doing was seducing his dashing and alluring compatriot. With all the hours they had spent together their friendship had deepened but their sensual intimacy had not grown in the least. He was certain Percival found him at least a fascinating specimen if not outright attractive. This morning it seemed Percival had awakened with a cockstand and commenced watching Bertram as he attended to his toilet. Flattering, to be sure, but was it, perchance, something more?

In the meantime, Bertram had been tormented by their closeness, knowing it would be boorish—or, rather, villainous—to coax the young marquess into a physical entanglement he was most assuredly not ready for. Still, Bertram wanted—no, *needed* to frig himself. He'd only managed the act last night after Percival's snoring signaled he slept soundly. While his deep slumber was a good sign he was starting to slough off the tribulations of his life back in England, Bertram resigned himself that he would have to wait to see if their relationship was ever going to be something more than just friends.

This afternoon was definitely not going to be the start of any new sensual journey. It was merely going to be the end of tiresome days spent sitting. His mind's wish to sleep off the boredom was juxtaposed with his body's aching need to walk. It did not matter where. Any distance longer than a train car or a station platform.

The summer heat of late afternoon slammed into him the moment he opened the door of the railway carriage. He and

Percival disembarked and, after nabbing a porter for their heavier bags, wended their way out the front of the small station where passengers and those expecting them milled about. On the cobblestones several conveyances were lined up, including a peasant's open wagon hitched to two oxen, a light two-wheeled dog cart, and a sleek four-wheeled coupé. Panic roiled through Bertram.

Oh, God, please not the wagon. That would be an indignity he could not endure at that moment.

On the pavement, Armand snapped his fingers, and harried porters began loading the wagon with their bags and boxes.

Percival sighed in relief. "If the wagon is for the luggage, I believe one of those carriages is for us."

Armand waved a greeting and came over. "My lords, I recommend you wait inside the station while we load the luggage. It will be much cooler. Once the wagon is underway, I will go ahead in the cart. You'll follow behind in the carriage. I should arrive before you." He glanced at the oxen. "I hope the luggage will arrive by this evening."

"How long a journey to the villa?" Percival asked Armand.

"I think perhaps not quite an hour."

Bertram kept his exasperation and displeasure in check. More traveling. At least it would be an hour with Percival at his side in the confined space of an elegant carriage.

In the meantime the two availed themselves of the toilets and the cooler air inside the station until Armand waved them over to the coupé where the driver stood by the open door.

Percival approached the driver. "Er, are you going to *Villa degli inglesi?*"

Amusement flitted over the driver's face, probably from Percival's mangled pronunciation. "*Si, signore.*"

"Thank you—"

"*Grazie.*" Bertram hoped he'd pronounced that passably well. The driver merely touched his cap and nodded.

Percival chuckled. "You'll have to teach me a few basic words, I think." He gestured to the leather upholstered interior with a slight bow. "After you, my lord viscount."

With enervated legs, Bertram climbed into the carriage. Moments later they were on the dusty road.

PERCIVAL STARED OUT the carriage's front and side windows at the panorama of the gorgeous Umbrian landscape. The golden rocks of hills rose above patches of green manicured farms. The breeze through the window was welcome in the summer heat. The carriage rattled, the noise of wheels rolling on dirt and stones filling the heavy silence between him and his seat-mate.

Bertram was tucked in his corner, lounging against the tufted leather, as if he had resigned himself to his lot as Percival's best friend—

Where had that thought come from? His own insecurities of rejection if he broached the subject of further intimacy?

Most likely Bertram was simply tired from the journey.

Percival was tired, as well. Exhausted, really. Hungry, too. But energized in a way he barely understood.

Because the man sitting at the other end of the carriage bench—not so very far away—was something more than merely his best friend.

And, yet, something not quite a lover.

Bertram inspired him in a way he barely understood. Inspired him with his stories, with his friendship, with his comforting presence over the last few days that had bordered on—dare he think it?—protection.

And inspired him with his supremely perfect body.

Percival had been with one man. A man who had seduced him without full assent. A man who had never loved him. Had never even been his friend.

But Bertram…

Percival shifted in his seat to give his burgeoning cock room in his trousers.

The carriage turned with the curve of the road, the new angle allowing the intense Italian afternoon sunlight to stream through the front window. Percival pulled down the front blinds against the glare.

Bertram growled a sigh. "Why the devil did you choose a place so far from civilization?"

The sensual baritone drew Percival back to the present. "It was recommended by one of my professors as a place for scholars of Etruscan history. It is far from civilization, I know," he admitted as the landscape became increasingly rural. "But the countryside is beautiful, as you can see. I do believe we will find much more to explore after we are rested." A good night's rest. "Perhaps tomorrow."

The smile Bertram turned on him set his heart quivering. "Then I look forward to tomorrow morning." The viscount angled a bit more toward Percival.

A sign? Did he dare make a move? How did one do such a thing? Did one simply act on one's desires?

How would he know Bertram wanted him as well?

A flush overtook him as his lungs constricted, making it difficult to breath normally. They were alone. In close quarters. They were going to be together for weeks, months…who knew?

"So," Bertram said softly, "we'll be alone in the middle of nowhere?"

Percival gulped.

Now. It had to be now.

He slowly inched along the soft leather bench. "Just two Englishmen."

"A valet and some peasants." Bertram leaned forward, planting his palm on the bench. An invitation?

Percival's heart pounded as he continued his slide along the seat. Shallow breaths left him lightheaded as he came face-to-face with Bertram, gliding his fingers over his outstretched, welcoming hand.

He hovered over Bertram's mouth, the viscount's hot breaths teasing his lips.

Now.

Percival dived in, pressing his lips to Bertram's, which parted slowly after a grunt of astonishment. He delved his tongue inside the viscount's mouth, tasting him, the scrape of afternoon stubble invigorating. Bertram leaned into Percival, kissing him back for only a moment before gripping his shoulders and pulling him off.

"Percy, we must be discreet," he hissed. He reached for the side window blinds, pulling each down. "England is unforgiving in its own right, but we are in a foreign country, a Catholic country, and need to be even more cautious."

The view of the rural Italian landscape now obscured, the carriage interior was dimmed considerably. Bertram's breath panted against his cheek, in rhythm to his own throbbing heart. Percival sought and pecked at the willing lips, wrapping his arms around Bertram's neck, climbing on top of his lap, straddling him as he continued to suck and sip at his mouth.

The heat of Bertram's crotch seeped through his trousers, teasing his stones, stiffening his already iron-hard cock. Bertram's prick swelled and pressed against the cleft of his buttocks. Percival rubbed and rocked, the rhythm of the carriage an erotic facilitator, each movement taking him closer to the edge of ecstasy.

Too soon, the clip-clop of the horses waned as the carriage slowed. With a gasp and a groan, Bertram pulled away, and urged Percival back to his side of the bench.

In the darkened space echoed the sounds of hands brushing and tugging fabric.

Bertram cleared his throat. "If we were man and woman, likely the coachman would expect us to exit disheveled. But as we are two men, we should look as if we were merely napping at most."

Percival worked at setting his own clothes aright as Bertram raised the side blinds. Each slunk in his own corner as the coach stopped.

The door opened and a young, dark-haired man dressed in simple peasant attire gestured for them to descend. Bertram faltered on the carriage step, the young man helping him gain his balance on the crushed gravel drive.

"*Merci*, pardon me, *grazie*," he mumbled. The young man nodded and helped Percival alight.

A handful of servants, neat and prim, stood outside the entrance of the three-story stone villa. Armand beckoned from the exquisitely carved entry portal.

Side by side Percival and Bertram entered the villa, both pausing in the foyer to immerse themselves in the cool air.

"If you will follow me, my lords," said Armand, "I will show you to your respective rooms. I do not know when your luggage will arrive," he added with a touch of exasperation. "However, you will find the housekeeper has provided a small repast to sustain you until supper."

Armand guided their way along a foyer and corridor richly decorated with etchings, ceramics, and painted plaster. They climbed the central staircase and turned right down a corridor.

He gestured to one door. "This is for Viscount Ravensburgh."

"Thank you, Armand," Bertram said before casting a wistful glance Percival's way, then escaping into his room.

"And this, my lord Norrington, is your room."

Right next to Bertram's. Might there be adjoining doors? Percival held that thought at bay as he thanked Armand then entered.

Afternoon light spilled through partially opened windows despite the halfway drawn blinds. The room was so unlike anything in England. White plaster walls extended up to a dark wood-beamed ceiling, with delicate floral painted decorations on the upper walls and between the beams. The furniture was seemingly from the previous century, refined and graceful with intricate inlaid patterns. On a desk near a window was laid a simple meal of bread, cheese, olives, and what appeared to be dried figs. A carafe of water and one of wine rounded out the offering.

A quick glance around the room revealed there was not a door between his and Bertram's room. Ah, well, he'd see him later, perhaps at supper. For now, though, Percival really needed to rest, a short nap at least. Perhaps after availing himself of some of the food.

He picked up an olive and stared out at the view from the window. The green valley rolled until it met the rocky promontory crowned by the town of Orvieto.

Sleepy contentment melted into a smile. What a lovely place to indulge in romantic notions of one's best friend.

CHAPTER SIX

Not every shore remains unexplored, but not every man has explored every shore. There will always be something new over the horizon.
— *The Adventures of Paolo the Pirate Hunter*

Umbria, Italy

As he stood on the villa's terrace overlooking the green plains of Umbria, Percival inhaled the morning air. *Ah, freedom.* He lifted his face to the sunshine and let out a long breath before bracing his hands on the stone wall skirting the edge. He leaned forward to admire the magnificent view. Perhaps he should consider a future here in sunny Italy, rather than dreary England.

He sighed then returned to his seat at the tile-top table laden with a simple breakfast. Dreary England was, unfortunately, his destiny. But for now, this moment, he was here in Italy and he should enjoy it.

And be as daring and bold as he had been yesterday afternoon in the carriage. He'd slept like a top last night, or as Byron put it, like the dead. Not just out of exhaustion from the rail journey, but from enervation after having spent all his energy on the courage to kiss Bertram.

His Bertie.

But now in the light of day—even after a refreshing slumber—discomfiture was setting in. He hadn't seen Bertram since their parting in the corridor leading to their respective bedrooms. And the viscount hadn't yet shown up for breakfast.

Perhaps he got lost. The grounds and the house were rather extensive.

Or decided to break his fast somewhere else.

"I missed you last night."

The rumble of Bertram's luscious baritone against his ear shattered his melancholia, the light puff of breath against his neck stirring sensual euphoria. Percival looked up to see his companion groomed and well-dressed as if going on an outing in London. So handsome, so perfect.

Percival tugged the tie at the waist of his dressing gown. He was dressed underneath, well mostly, but rather casually. It *was* Italy, for goodness sake. "Ah, so you went down to supper."

"A wonderful bean soup," Bertram said as he took the other chair at the table, "with more of that crusty bread from the tray in the room."

"That bread was so tasty, wasn't it? Or I was just hungry. I ate a bit of the meal, then I fear I fell asleep." Percival took a sip of coffee. "I must have slept for twelve hours. I woke up at dawn." He gazed at the view. "I never wake up at dawn."

Bertram chuckled. "A few days on a train with you and I do already know that particular quirk of yours."

He shot a quick grimace. "I recommend waking at dawn to witness the sunrise at least once while we are here. The view from the terrace is, well, religious."

"The view is rather magnificent, my lord," Bertram agreed. "Even if this gorgeous scenery was all I experienced this entire excursion, I would be grateful to you for your invitation. And," Bertram began with a grin as he poured himself a cup of coffee, "as I often wake early, that will not be a problem." He added a generous pour of warm milk then sat back, cradling his cup. "I surmise you missed the mist that hovers in the valley before sunrise. So the sunrise you say you witnessed was quite a bit after dawn."

Percival chuckled. He thought as much. He really did never wake at dawn.

"After supper last night," continued Bertram, "I visited the library. Several well-worn club chairs and sofas. The stacks of books on the tables and desks seemed almost curated, as if chosen for someone." He took a long swallow. "And yet we seem to be the only visitors here."

"Ah, yes, we are. Professor Bellamy and his colleagues are traveling south to Rome, then to Naples. I think perhaps to Sicily as well. So we are here alone. He said it seemed silly to dismiss the staff for the weeks he is gone. I have sublet the villa from him."

"Wouldn't you rather be here with Professor Bellamy at the same time? You could discuss the Etruscans and whatever else it is scholars discuss."

"Which might include some inquiries about why I left during Easter term and will be absent all of Trinity term." Percival shook his head. "I prefer to not be reminded of my past right now." He flicked his gaze in the viscount's direction. "I prefer to spend time with you," he admitted in a low voice.

Bertram carefully placed his cup in its saucer. "Percy, if I may remind you of one thing?" He met Percival's gaze. "I *am* your past."

"Yes, but you're the good part."

After a quiet exhalation, Bertram reached his hand out on the table. "Shall we discuss what happened in the carriage?"

Percival's heart pounded. "I was rather bold, was I not?" He could barely look at Bertram. "Too bold?"

"Anything you want to do to me, do with me, say to me, will never be too bold, Percy."

He gripped Bertram's hand, their palms melding, the warmth infusing him with a quiet comfort. "I'm grateful for your indulgence, Bertie. I'm still so new at this sort of thing."

"I know. And I'll wait."

BERTRAM SIGHED as Percival released his hold, the sensation of his touch lingering on his palm. Yes, he had napped from sheer exhaustion after their arrival at the villa, but fitfully. He simply could not forget the wonderment of Percival's attempted seduction.

He'd gone to supper hoping to find Percival, hoping perhaps they could somehow find a way to continue what had been started. But now, in the daylight, Percival's trepidation was apparent. Still, desire clearly persisted in the marquess, while it positively smoldered within Bertram.

"Try the cornettis." Percival pointed to a basket of what looked like croissants. "Some are filled with strawberry jam."

Bertram grabbed a *cornetto*. "You really did not bother learning any Italian, did you?"

"Not a word, unfortunately. Why do you ask?"

"*Cornetto* is the singular. More than one would be *cornetti* not cornettis."

Percival laughed. "Then it is a damn good thing I invited you on this journey. You will safeguard me from future faux pas."

"Ah, well, I only know a handful of words and a little grammar. I am utterly unreliable otherwise."

Beyond the basket of *cornetti*, papers were strewn over the tiled table. Bertram tilted his head to get a better look. Maps, books, and handwritten notes. "What's all this? Planning our excursion for today?"

"Professor Bellamy left me a packet with some information about our immediate area. Beyond seeing what he has suggested, though, I would love to simply explore the countryside—" he leaned toward Bertram "—in hopes of finding undiscovered Etruscan treasure."

"Of course, that's why we're here, is it not?"

"I had merely thought to see previous archaeological findings. Then I had a notion this morning—"

"At dawn."

"Yes, at dawn," Percival said with annoyance. "I had a notion about what if I discovered something new. Wouldn't that be wonderful?"

"Like if Paolo the Pirate Hunter stumbled upon a secret pirate lair."

Percival chuckled. "Yes. I'll be on an Etruscan hunting adventure." He grabbed another *cornetto*. "I do know such a possibility is highly unlikely. But I can dream, can't I?"

"I'm very glad you feel at ease enough to let your dreams conquer your fears."

"I am hoping to slough off that fear. That is one of the reasons for this adventure. I suppose no one even knows who I am over here."

Bertram patted his arm. "You're safe. Well, perhaps not from highwaymen and bandits—"

Percival laughed.

"But know you are safe with me."

"Thank you, Bertie." Percival became pensive as a crease formed between his brows.

"And you are also safe to express your fears out loud. I will listen. I'm not sure I can offer advice. But I can listen."

A tear slithered down Percival's cheek. "Thank you, Bertie. You are a good friend. I fear you are my sole friend."

"I cannot possibly be. There's cousin Nicholas, and I'm certain you have Oxford friends. Obviously, your Professor Bellamy is a sort of friend."

"Then I should say you are my best friend."

Bertram grinned as he studied Percival's face. He wiped the tear with his thumb.

"After breakfast, let's go have an adventure worthy of Paolo the Pirate Hunter."

CHAPTER SEVEN

"We have our orders, Captain. Is it prudent to be exploring parts
unknown while the pirate remains free?"
"Yes," Paolo said. "We might just uncover a villain wherever we
may be."
— *The Adventures of Paolo the Pirate Hunter*

From atop a knoll, Percival placed hands on hips and
surveyed the surrounding landscape. A wide-brimmed straw hat
shielded his eyes from the morning sunlight that bathed the farms
and low rolling hills in a golden hue. Bertram came up alongside
and he exhaled contentment.

A couple of days wandering in the countryside searching for
Etruscan treasure had been fruitless—well, fruitless only as far as
Etruscan treasures. Spending time with Bertram as his constant
companion had been quite satisfying. Bertram was game for any
adventure it seemed.

Unfortunately, Percival was not yet ready for life's biggest adventure after his heart had been thoroughly burned. But Bertram's constant presence was helping him heal.

After their first day exploring near the villa, Percival had arranged for a tour of the Etruscan necropolis on the north side of Orvieto. The next day, they had attended service at the glorious Gothic cathedral in town and afterward, ambled through narrow, medieval streets.

But now Percival was a little more determined to find something more ancient. Earlier that morning, after a filling breakfast, they had set out on foot to explore the countryside a little further afield.

"I know there are Etruscan treasures still waiting to be found in these hills, Bertie."

Bertram glanced over at Percival, the viscount's amusement apparent in the shadow of his own wide-brimmed hat. "Perhaps we'll get lost and discover some ancient pots."

"That sounds positively delightful. I'll return to Oxford and be thought a hero by the students of classical archaeology."

"And if we find nothing?"

Percival sighed. "I'll take my exams in obscurity."

"You could further your studies at Cambridge," Bertram suggested with one eyebrow arched tauntingly.

The preposterous notion set him to laughing. "Oh, please, you can't possibly be suggesting that, truly?"

Bertram chuckled. "Spoken like a true Oxonian." He gazed at the fields below dotted with peasants bent over, working. "By the way, if we get lost, did you ever bother to learn any Italian?"

"No." He'd been using evocative gestures to communicate with the staff and townspeople. "But I have a full command of Latin."

Bertram let out a sharp guffaw. "Well, if we come upon Julius Caesar and his legions, I will rely upon your expert translation skills to get us out of danger."

The remark got the look of disdain it deserved. "Let us push on."

"Yes, let's." Bertram brushed Percival's right hand then grasped it briefly, before proceeding down the hill as if nothing had happened. The simple act stirred up a flutter of sensations within.

He wanted so much to be able to hold hands as they sauntered over rock and grass. But more than that, he really wanted to kiss Bertram again.

"I wish we could hold hands," he said aloud.

Bertram stopped and turned toward him. "It is maddening, is it not?"

"And kissing. I'd like to be able to kiss you."

"I would greatly enjoy that. But we really should not be freely exhibiting our affections in a foreign land."

Percival considered the gleam in Bertram's eye. "You're being clever, aren't you?"

"I am," he admitted with a sigh.

"But when a woman may wrap her arm around a man's and lean her head against his shoulder in the broad light of day, it contrasts starkly to how we must be so utterly prudent."

"It does." Bertram offered a thin smile. "As best friends we may wrap our arms about each other's shoulders."

"I suppose." Percival cast his gaze on the rocky ground. "Still, I'd really like to kiss you again. I like kissing. I never got to do much of it with…well, before."

"I'd like that very much. Perhaps I could sneak into your bedroom at night?"

He looked up, startled at the suggestion. *Oh, yes, oh yes, please.* "And I would like *that* very much."

Bertram reached out and draped his arm across Percival's shoulder. "I'll keep that in mind." He grinned. "Shall we continue our explorations?"

They scrambled over boulders, their shoes wholly inadequate for such exertions, their athletic bodies ably supporting their efforts.

The heat of the midday sun impelled them to unbutton waistcoats and remove jackets. Armand had insisted they wear the wide-brimmed straw hats from the collection left at the villa purposely for tourists. For some segments of their walk, the brims were the only shade they had. The valet had also insisted they each carry a satchel with a canteen of water plus a meal of bread and cheese.

They climbed to the top of a low hill upon which stood an ancient and twisted oak tree.

"Let's rest here a bit, my lord."

"Really, Bertie, you have to stop calling me that." Percival picked a rock to lean against and set down his satchel. "Especially when we are alone in a foreign country. No one knows who we are."

"And since we do not know Italian well enough, we cannot convey the intricacies of the English aristocratic system to anyone."

Bertram's droll tone sparked Percival to snicker.

They sat in comfortable silence as they shared bread and cheese and cool drinking water in the shade. Still, the potently male presence at Percival's side was flustering.

"Bertie," he dared, "how did you know about me? I mean how I am…how I like men."

"I suppose because I was just like you, so I could tell from how you acted. It was a conclusion based mostly on observation but also my own feelings, if that makes any sense."

"It does, I think." Now that he better understood such things.

"And Jack, well, he was a little more forthright in his predilections. Perhaps because he is—" Bertram cleared his throat, "was one year older. But all along, even while I suspected you were like me and Jack, I had no ulterior motives for friendship. I just thought of you as a boy with a wonderful imagination. Jack felt otherwise, I suppose."

"And swooped down upon me."

Bertram winced. "I should have protected you."

The confession warmed Percival. "I have never thought you—or Nicky, for that matter—should have been my savior. You are blameless. Jack was a villain through and through. If I had not been his victim, there would have been another."

The warmth of Bertram's hand surrounding his startled him.

"I am humbled by your fortitude, Percy. I still feel so much anger, and yet you seem to have come to terms with the situation."

"I've had a lot of time alone to think. In fact, my life with Jack was all I could think about at times."

Bertram squeezed his hand. "I remind you I'm always willing to listen should you need someone to talk to."

"Thank you, Bertie." Percival released his hand. "For the moment, I think a relaxing snooze in this balmy weather is in order, don't you think?"

"I hear the Italians do not work in the middle of the day under the hot sun," Bertram said as he stretched out and closed his eyes. "But rather rest until late afternoon when it is cooler."

"I think I could get used to that sort of life."

"Yes, but then they work until evening."

With a chuckle Percival extended himself alongside Bertram. "Shall we join them in their custom?"

Bertram opened one eye to glare at the marquess. "I already have."

His chuckle released into a long exhale. Minutes later, joy burbled within at the sound of Bertram's rhythmic breathing at his side.

Bertram awoke with only one notion on his mind.

A pressing need to relieve himself.

Percival was no longer at his side. He glanced around, spying the marquess with his back to him beside a rock.

Apparently he had awakened to the same notion.

Bertram sidled up alongside as Percival was buttoning his fly. He aimed at the spot on the ground wet from Percival's efforts. "Might as well soil only a small portion of the landscape."

A deep, sharp bark came from behind. Bertram finished and buttoned up as quickly as possible.

Before them stood a farmer, wrinkled and grizzled, short and muscular. At his side was a large dog, its thick white coat yellowed and dirty. Both had heads cocked as if in curiosity. The dog yipped once again then sat, satisfied from a job well done. The farmer grinned.

Bertram smiled back.

"*Buongiorno*," said the farmer.

Bertram poked Percival. "*Buongiorno*."

"What does that mean?" Percival whispered.

"Good day in Italian."

Percival made an attempt at the greeting.

"*Inglesi?*"

Unsurprisingly, the farmer had ascertained they were English.

"*Oui*," Percival blurted in the only continental language he knew fluently.

Bertram laughed. "*Sì*," he responded with a nod.

The dog got up and sauntered over to Bertram then sat at his side. Bertram gave it a pat on the head.

The farmer continued to smile, showing a little bit of yellowed teeth.

Percival leaned in. "Can you ask him if there are any Etruscan ruins and potsherds around here?" he said still in a whisper.

"How do you say Etruscan in Italian? Or potsherd?"

"I haven't a clue. Didn't you just make a study of the language?"

"I didn't get that far in my vocabulary."

The farmer watched them as they spoke, his face pinched as if he were trying to understand them, as if he could understand a bit of what they were saying.

Percival exhaled slowly. "Maybe it's similar to the Latin, *Etrusca,* or French *étrusque.* And the area they lived in was called Etruria. Well, that's what we call it in English, I can't imagine it's so different in Italian."

Bertram would have to try his best. *"Ci sono rovine,* er, *étrusque*—" the French would have to do "—*in questo luogo?"*

Percival nudged him. "What did you ask?"

"If there are any Etruscan ruins in this place." At least he hoped that was what he said.

The farmer nodded enthusiastically. *"Si, si."* The man continued to speak to them rapidly as if they might understand him, gesticulating with prodigious energy, his grin deepening the lines on his face.

Bertram smiled politely while struggling to glean a word or two in the speedy stream of Italian. Perhaps something about a monument? Or stones? Both?

"Etruscan," Percival exclaimed. "I would swear he said Etruscan." He stared at the farmer as if he could understand. *"Etrusco.* That's it. *Etrusco."* He repeated the word with reverence, as if it were a prayer.

The farmer beamed and nodded. *"Etrusco."*

"How fortuitous," murmured Bertram.

"Venite," said the farmer indicating that they should follow him.

Bertram met Percival's gaze. "Shall we follow?"

Percival flashed a grin. "Oh, absolutely. I'll pack up." An excited glimmer shone in the marquess's blue eyes.

A surprising response. "You're rather trusting, my lord."

"One only lives once, my dear viscount. Taking chances is the only way one will truly live a well-considered life."

Bertram chuckled. The change was welcome. Perhaps being in Italy or, he hoped, Percival's spending time with him had prompted this development.

They followed the old farmer and his dog along some rarely trodden path, over rocks, through shrubs and gnarled trees, to the top of an unkempt grassy mound. The farmer indicated they should wait. Down the hill was a view of fields where peasants made their way with their burdens of crops toward already well-laden donkey carts.

While the dog stood sentinel by Percival and Bertram, the farmer scuttled down the mound, disappearing for a moment seemingly inside the small hill. He reappeared and shouted up to them with a wave. *"Venite."*

They scrambled over rocks and grasses. The farmer grinned as he stood on the top step of a stone staircase leading down to a grotto shrouded in the long shadows of afternoon.

Percival gasped. "An Etruscan crypt."

"Not a cavern filled with highwaymen and thieves?"

The marquess scowled at him. "Please. I've only just become a trusting soul. Don't destroy this moment for me."

The old man held up a lantern inside of which was a well-used candle thick with drips of wax, the flame bright. He offered the lantern to Percival and gestured that the two should enter, while he would wait, the dog sitting obediently at his side.

"After you," said Bertram.

As if descending into the Underworld, they slowly climbed down the stairs, not mere slabs of stone, but steps carved into the living rock. At the bottom they were assaulted with a rush of frigid air. They stepped further inside.

Sunlight lingered at the entrance, helping to brighten their view a little. A cavernous space the size of an aristocrat's drawing room was entirely carved in the rock. They stood in a sort of foyer with stone benches clinging to the walls, separated from the main space by a series of severe columns. Beyond the columns the larger room was covered in murals depicting an ancient fête, where participants reclined on couches holding wine cups while watching dancers flanking a painted doorway at the far end. On the opposite end of the foyer another entrance mirrored the one they had just used, except this one was filled with rubble as if the mound on top had partially collapsed.

Bertram stood wide-eyed, taking in everything. He'd never before witnessed such a sight.

Percival placed the lantern on a bench. "My God, it is positively icy down here."

"The Etruscans seemed to have created a way to honor their dead while gaining respite from the oppressive heat."

"And perhaps take a moment to celebrate their invention of such a cool space."

"Celebrate?"

"This is no mere catacomb, Bertie." Percival held his arms wide and spun around. "There is enough room down here to host a grand occasion for the living."

Bertram chuckled. "Thus spake the Oxford scholar of the dead."

Percival pointed to a basket with ceramic cups. "I do believe the modern Italians have figured out this very notion. I'm certain our farmer friend enjoys his luncheon here during the summer."

"The absence of dead bodies would make the space more attractive."

"Hmm." With a hand on his chin Percival surveyed the tomb. "There would have been sarcophagi and funerary urns. I suppose those were looted centuries ago."

He fished in his jacket pocket and took out a notebook and pencil and began sketching. He wandered around throwing the light from the lamp in every corner of the space, drafting views from various angles, examining the paintings and decorative carvings then quickly sketching, muttering exclamations and praise.

The Etruscans seemed to be an animated people who enjoyed life. Or perhaps simply enjoyed drinking. The paintings showed happy men and women reclining on couches holding cups while nude adolescents served them what was probably wine from elegant ewers. The bent arms and legs of the dancers on the far wall indicated joyous movement. Despite years of dust, the greens, blues, reds, and yellows of the ancient murals were still bold.

After a spell, Bertram sat on a carved stone bench, waiting and watching. The paintings and the sculpture were amazing, but even more so was the ecstatic expression on Percival's face. The wonderment reflected in his visage brightened the space more than the dull glow of the lamp. His focus was attractive, his lithe movements, crouching and bobbing like one of the dancers, were arousing.

Finally, with a deep sigh, Percival folded up his notebook and placed it and his pencil in his jacket, giving the pocket a little tap.

"This was incredible. We should pay the man."

"Oh, very definitely," agreed Bertram.

They emerged from the crypt, lowering their brims to shield their eyes from the now too-bright sun.

The farmer clapped his hands together. "*Buono? Buono?*"

"Very *buono*, my good sir," Percival said with a nod and a shake of the farmer's hand. "*Grazie.*" He took out his coin purse and opened it.

"*No, prego, no.*" This was accompanied by open palms slicing the air. He pointed to the fields and pantomimed a pulling action, then grasped Bertram's and Percival's hands.

"I think he wants us to do a bit of farming," said Bertram.

"That's your bailiwick."

"It is," Bertram responded with a laugh. "Shall we?"

"But of course."

They descended the hill to the farm, where a cacophonous array of activities abounded. The farmer's large white dog joined the chickens who milled about unfettered. A few women, young and old, carried large baskets filled with clothing, then proceeded to hang laundry. In a field, workmen scythed tall grasses.

"Voi, prego, venite," said the farmer as he gestured to the field.

They followed the farmer. He bade them stop as he went to speak with a workman. The farmer gestured wildly and characteristically as the field hand nodded in comprehension. The farmer then waved them over and they joined him.

He knelt before a stack of cut grass. No, not grass. Grain. Bertram picked up a stalk and met the farmer's eager gaze. "Wheat?"

The farmer grinned and nodded. *"Si, grano."*

"Grano," Bertram echoed.

"Si, osservate." Watch.

The farmer scooped up a generous bunch of stalks with one hand, then a smaller cluster with the other hand. He wrapped the smaller cluster around the large bunch, tying it together.

Percival reached for the newly tied bundle, his eyes wide. "A sheaf of wheat. I have never in my life seen one in actuality." He stroked it, eyes focused as if mesmerized. "I have seen its depiction in art, but never the original source. It is the symbol of Demeter, although I suppose since we are in Italy, I should call her Ceres according to Roman mythology."

The farmer smiled and nodded, probably not comprehending. Or perhaps he did?

"Shall we help make sheaves, then?" Bertram asked.

"Oh, most definitely." Percival appeared quite eager about the prospect.

Bertram stripped off his jacket and unbuttoned his waistcoat. "You've never worked with your hands before, have you?"

Percival scoffed. "I'm a marquess who's spent the last few years cloistered from the world. Although I did do my fair share of digging in the dirt on the St. Albans estate when I was a child. I'll manage."

They tossed aside their satchels and joined the workmen in the field. Bundling took dexterity and finesse, skills they had to learn swiftly as the scythe men were fast and the grain piled up quickly.

Their bundles of wheat—*fasci* as the farmer called them— once finished, were stacked together, grain ends up, in a pyramid. Bertram had seen such structures in the fields of Hertfordshire but only now understood how the stacks were actually made. Intense physical labor resulting in cut and cramped hands.

The afternoon went quickly, and, despite the hard work, enjoyably. Bertram amused himself by snatching peeks at Percival stripped to his shirt, sleeves rolled up, the placket entirely unbuttoned.

A fetching sight to behold.

As evening descended, burnishing the gold of sunlight with a rosy hue, a short and pudgy middle-aged woman arrived, speaking loudly and rapidly to the farmer, the large white dog in tow.

"The farmer's wife?" Bertram guessed.

"May I never have one."

Bertram laughed. "As you'll never be a farmer, you're safe."

An invitation to supper was conveyed via pantomime. Some of the workmen waved and departed, others joined Bertram and Percival as they followed the farmer and his presumed wife to a two-story stone farmhouse. A couple of girls and an old woman led goats and mules into the stables on the ground floor, the dog now at their heels.

At a water pump near a trough, the men washed faces, arms, and hands. Bertram was grateful for the cool water against his sweat- and dust-covered skin and aching muscles. He and Percival dressed as best they could for dinner, straightening shirts and waistcoats, finger combing their hair, donning their jackets.

They grabbed their satchels and climbed a stone staircase on the outside of the farmhouse to the first floor. They were invited to sit at the benches on either side of a large, rough-hewn wooden table in the center of what appeared to be a kitchen. They sat side by side, and the rest of the household took their places around them. The farmer stood at one end of the table where sat two square, flat loaves of bread and two pitchers in the same shape as the ewers depicted in the Etruscan murals. The wife took her place at the other end before a rustic tureen and a stack of bowls.

The farmer said a few words. Bertram tried his best to comprehend, fairly certain the farmer was asking their names.

"*Come mi chiamo?*" he asked. The farmer nodded.

Bertram smiled. "*Mi chiamo Bertram e il nome del mio amico è Percy.*"

Percival nudged him with a raised brow.

"My name is Bertram and my friend here is Percy," Bertram repeated for the marquess's benefit.

"*Mi chiamo Donato Rossi.*" The farmer placed his hand on his heart. "*Benvenuti a casa nostra.*"

"The farmer's name is Donato Rossi and he welcomes us to his home," Bertram said to Percival. The farmer then went around the table and introduced those present in too rapid a pace for Bertram to completely understand. The three workmen were his sons or perhaps sons of a relation, Agnolo, Jacopo, and Ugo. The two girls were his daughters; the eldest was Belda, and the younger one was Giana. The older woman was his mother or perhaps his mother-in-law and she was called Nonna, which really just meant "grandmother". The middle-aged woman was indeed his wife, Stefania, or rather, Signora Rossi. The dog, patiently curled up in a corner, was aptly named Orso.

"Orso?" Percival quietly asked Bertram. "Is that like the Latin, *ursus?*"

"Yes. Orso indeed means bear."

Rossi picked up one of the loaves of bread and murmured what seemed to be a prayer. He smiled at Bertram and Percival. "*Grano,*" he pointed toward the field where they had just worked, "*fa il pane.*" He held up the bread.

"Wheat makes bread," Percival said.

All those around them smiled, Giana giggled, while her elder sister Belda was apparently moonstruck now Percival had spoken.

Thence commenced the supper of hearty boar stew with thick chunks of bread, all washed down with cool water and plenty of wine. Conversation was conveyed via gestures, sketches by Percival, and laughter. Giana, perhaps ten or eleven years old, stared at the two guests as if they were exotic figures from a fantastical world, while Belda, probably around sixteen years of age, revealed a spark of interest in her eyes whenever she espied Percival. The marquess, of course, was his charming self, telling stories in Latin, English, and something that might have passed for Italian but perhaps was Spanish. Maybe Portuguese. Definitely mixed with French.

In a situation such as this, no perceived threats or judgments, Percival shone like the bright star of the aristocracy he was, exhibiting a confidence that should never have been quashed by a villain such as Jack.

PERCIVAL FINISHED HIS wine then stared at the cup. A small, dark ceramic vessel that fit perfectly in his palm. So simple, or, rather, so uncomplicated.

So unlike his life.

He'd not had nightly suppers with his mother and father since he had been a child. Those evenings had been excruciatingly formal, but the three of them had been together, at least. There had been conversation as well as lessons—in etiquette, in deportment, and, if one could read between the lines of their dialogue, lessons about life. Subtext was complicated, though. Percival had to be sharp at family meals, he could not simply relax and enjoy as these Italian peasants did.

A clattering perked him up. Supper was finished and the dishes were being cleared. One by one each family member rose and bid good night to their pater while Rossi nodded his blessing. As each left, they also bowed to Bertram and Percival.

Belda lingered, looking up demurely from lowered lids, her lips curving into a smile, bashfulness barely concealing her excitement about something. She gestured toward the door indicating they should follow her, then grabbed a lantern.

"I suppose we are to spend the night," murmured Bertram. "It is far too dark to find our way back to the villa. Will Armand be overly concerned at our disappearance?"

"I imagine word will get out about the *inglesi* who helped a farmer with his wheat and he'll figure it out."

Bertram chuckled. "Well, then, the adventure continues. After you, Percy."

Percival followed Belda as she led the way into the darkening night. Under the light of the half-moon and the pale glow of the lantern they quietly trod down the stairs, Bertram seemingly slowing his steps in time with Percival's, as if being protective. Percival warmed inside at the sentiment.

At the bottom of the stairs, Belda turned into the stables on the ground floor. Were they to sleep with the goats and mules?

Percival had to stifle a chuckle at the utter romance of the idea.

Once inside the stable, the sleeping quarters became apparent. Belda showed them to an alcove—perhaps used by a workman upon occasion or pilgrims such as they—separated from the main area by curtains and a surrounding half-wall. Against the inside of the stuccoed outer wall was a bed—not a narrow bed for one, nor a double bed for two. Something in-between. And rather sturdy looking, with heavy posts and cross braces. A thick mattress, feather pillows, and a quilt that may have been quite elegant fifty years earlier, completed the setting.

It all looked quite comfortable. And Percival was suddenly feeling very tired.

"*Signor* Bertram," said Belda pointing to the bed. "*Dormire qui.*"

Bertram lifted a brow in Percival's direction. "So we are to sleep apart. I shall see you in the morning." He turned to the girl and offered a bow. "*Grazie, Signorina Rossi.* I am very much obliged."

If Bertram was in the stables, wherever was Percival to sleep? The wood shed?

Belda lit another lamp and handed it to Bertram. She then turned to Percival and offered a shy smile as she held out her hand.

Percival took her hand and she led him out of the barn back into the moonlight.

They circled around the farmhouse, to the back side, the pale stonework of the house reflecting the light of the lamp and moon. A door at the far end was the only shadow to break the otherwise uninterrupted wall. A back door of sorts, but to the ground floor.

Belda held a finger to her lips then lifted the metal door latch and led him inside, closing the door behind them.

The room was small, spartan, but with every necessity. A table, a chair, a wardrobe. A bed took up most of the space, the headboard and footboard decorated with rough carved vegetal motifs. Belda put the lamp on the table, then went to Percival and slid her fingers up his lapels to his shoulders. She tugged, indicating he should take off his jacket.

He began to at the same moment she began unbuttoning her bodice.

Panic roiled his stomach. He shot a glance at the bed. Did she mean…did she expect…?

Good God.

"Belda."

She looked at him, her elation crinkling to displeasure when she saw he had not begun to undress.

Percival thought fast. "No. I simply cannot," he said. He placed both his hands on his heart and widened his eyes soulfully. He undulated his right hand and arm as if waves on an ocean, his left hand thumping against his heart mimicking its passionate beating. With the index finger of his right hand, he drew a circle around the fourth finger of his left hand.

Her mouth fell open. She rebuttoned her bodice in a haphazard manner.

Percival sighed in relief that she understood his pantomime.

"I shall join *Signor* Bertram." He pointed to the door.

She nodded quickly.

Once outside in the cool night air, Percival exhaled. Without aid of a lamp, moonlight was his only guide around the house to the stables.

Luckily the lamp left for Bertram still burned, aiding his way as he approached.

Bertram, dressed in shirt and drawers, was hanging up his trousers on a peg along the wall.

"*Bertie,*" Percival whispered.

Bertram turned in his direction, surprise melting into suspicion. "Not a rat-infested cellar, I hope?"

Percival chuckled. "Nothing of the sort. She offered me a comfortable bed. The problem was she was going to be in it as well as I."

Bertram laughed quietly. "And what happened?"

"I was gripped by a wave of nausea."

"That bad."

"Bertie, I have no inclination to sleep with a woman ever. I am positively dreading the moment when I am expected to produce an heir."

"I suppose you'll figure something out by then."

"I suppose. I hope it won't be for ages yet."

"You didn't insult our hostess, did you?"

"Hardly. Through wordless theatrics, I implied my heart was true to my fiancée back home in England."

Bertram chuckled. "So you intend to join me?"

At this point he had no choice, but... "Well, I could sleep in the hay."

"Percy..." It was said with a touch of scolding.

"Do you mind?"

"Not at all." Bertram slid under the covers and pressed his back to the wall, making a sliver of space. "I'm utterly exhausted. Could you douse the lamp before you settle in?"

Percival undressed quickly, his cock burgeoning with the shedding of each garment. Surely Bertram would know?

Luckily the rest of his body was exhausted. He'd get some sleep, but he wouldn't be able to control his dreams.

CHAPTER EIGHT

"Remain calm, yet vigilant. The villain may strike at any moment."
— *The Adventures of Paolo the Pirate Hunter*

Percival awoke, the bright light of day streaming through diaphanous curtains, a newly laid fire crackling in the grate. Surroundings so familiar yet so completely unexpected—

Panic flooded over him. Something was terribly wrong. Terribly wrong.

What the devil was he doing in Jack's bedroom?

He should get up, leave, escape. *Now.*

But he couldn't move. He was trapped, his limbs paralyzed, immobile under an arm draped heavily over his, pinning him on his side, the body behind him pressed into his, its cock jabbing his nether region, its cruel intention apparent. Any movement would awaken his captor, with unwelcome repercussions—

A rooster crowed, hauling Percival out of his nightmare and into reality.

His heart raced as he lay wide-eyed and looked around.

Italy. The stables. A bed shared with Bertram.

The viscount's arm was wrapped around him, as if holding him in an embrace, his morning erection nestled in the cleft of Percival's buttocks.

His friend harbored no cruel intentions. On the contrary. There was something bordering on the romantic about the whole situation. If there were no possibility of the farmer's daughters finding them, well, then, they could spend a moment snuggling…

Except terror curdled in his gut.

Damn it! Why the hell did Jack still invade his thoughts?

Percival ripped himself out of bed, wiping tears of frustration as he stumbled toward his clothes hanging on pegs on the wall.

Bertram awoke and looked around, then landed a dazed expression at Percival, before blushing. "I apologize. It's morning, you were in bed with me and I was dreaming. A rather erotic dream, I must admit." He got up and adjusted his crotch.

"Were you dreaming about me?" Percival asked quietly.

"I think so," he said with an uneven smile. "Rather non-specific, I have to say. Yes, you were there, but you weren't there. You know how dreams can be?"

"I do," Percival muttered. "I apologize. I didn't mean to startle you. It's just that…" He drew in a steadying breath. "Jack used to pin me down in the morning," he blurted. "Then he would…" He couldn't say it.

Bertram emitted a strangled gasp. He remained motionless, a deathly pallor marring his face. "I'm so very sorry, Percy. I…" He swept his hand through his hair then grabbed his trousers. With back turned, he quickly dressed.

Percival did the same, mortification and confusion pulsing through him.

The deep woof of the dog Orso announced the arrival of the farmer Rossi.

"*Buongiorno.*" He pointed upstairs. "*Colazione?*"

Percival threw Bertram a questioning look.

"He wishes us good morning and is inviting us to breakfast."

"I…I just want to go back home. I mean to the villa."

"I understand. I'll thank him and let him know we need to return. I hope I can convey as much."

While Bertram conversed with Rossi, Percival finished dressing and made sure he had all of his notebooks in his satchel.

After polite goodbyes, and provisioned with bread and cheese from Nonna Rossi and full canteens from the pump, they walked back to the villa. The morning sunlight was a cheery shade of pale gold, and not intense enough to slow them down with its heat. They did not say much along the way, although there was so much to talk about. Percival was still quite distressed by the morning's apparition.

As they walked up the hill, the delicate bell tower crowning the red tile roof came into view.

Home. Well, a place of respite and comfort anyway.

"I want to soak in a hot bath for a while." He needed to wash away far more than just dust and sweat.

Bertram chuckled. "That sounds like an excellent idea. You have yours first and I will wait. I don't want to wear the servants out running up and down stairs."

Percival smiled. Bertram was truly a kind, generous person. But he needed to be apart from him for a while. He needed to collect himself.

He needed to make sure that any future sensual encounters with the viscount would be devoid of any association with his nemesis.

~ INTERLUDE ~

The Adventures of Paolo the Pirate Hunter, the Magnificent Adventurer, who, along with his First Mate Barnaby, Protects the Seas from the Evil Pirate Jonas the Marauder

by Bertram Atherley, The Right Honorable 2nd Viscount Ravensburgh

Barnaby cupped his hands around his metal tankard as if to protect the ale within. But he wasn't at the public house to protect his drink.

He was there to protect the innocent.

Paolo had sent him on a mission to uncover which of the various pirate gangs who called Nassau Town home was impressing boys barely out of leading strings into Jonas the Marauder's dastardly corps. With his golden blond curls and piercing blue eyes, Paolo himself was too well known in these parts to pose as spy. But Barnaby had the sort of face no one remembered and a fiery anger just as strong as his captain's.

"Yuh lookin' fer work?"

Barnaby smelled the pirate before he elbowed alongside.

"Maybe."

"My ship needs good strong men, an' yuh look like yuh needs the work."

"What kind of ship?" Barnaby drummed his fingers against his tankard, the rhythm allaying his tension.

"Frigate."

"How many aboard?"

"Ten."

Barnaby kept his oath to himself. A ship like that required dozens of men. "Small crew."

"Ten what's worth mentionin'. Ship's got a good size crew."

"I don't work slave ships." Barnaby took a swig of ale.

"Got no slaves."

Barnaby took another draught from his tankard. "I don't work on ships where the crew's been murdered or deserted either."

"We gotta recruit at every port. Pay is good and some stay to whore and gamble."

"Whoring and gambling sound like better alternatives."

"If yuh got money. Yuh don' look like you's got money."

Barnaby and Paolo had purposely chosen his costume so he appeared as a down and out sailor. He guzzled the rest of his ale. "I don't. Buy me another and we'll talk."

Not a minute later his tankard had been filled.

"I needs ten more men."

"That only makes twenty."

"Yuh got some learnin' in yuh, huh? There's some kids what's got fealty to the cap'n. They make up the rest."

Eureka. "I need to check out the ship first. Where's it docked?"

"West end of the harbor. Ship's *The Jack Tar*. Ask for ole Bart when yuh get there. That's me."

Barnaby raised his tankard. "Will do."

He kept his smile of triumph to himself. He and Paolo would celebrate their victory once the boys were safe.

CHAPTER NINE

A first mate anticipates his captain's needs, whatever those needs
may be.
— *The Adventures of Paolo the Pirate Hunter*

Umbria, Italy, the next morning

Bertram stared at his breakfast of scrambled eggs with
truffles, curls of sheep's cheese atop grilled flat bread, and a bowl
of cherries. Every morsel would be delectable. But without
Percival as his dining companion, there would be significantly less
flavor to the meal.

He unfolded the days' old London *Times*, a subscription
Professor Bellamy had continued despite not being at the villa, and
commenced his solitary repast. The words on the page soon
blurred as his thoughts wandered.

Ever since yesterday's horror of Percival waking up and
thinking him Jack, Bertram had been rendered morose. Even a
pleasant soak in the tub could not erase the alarm nor disentangle

the snarl of emotions. He himself had been enjoying a sensual dream, but that his pleasure had dredged up panic within Percival left him sickened. He hadn't seen the marquess since their return to the villa, and had been informed by Armand that Percival had left early that morning.

"With his satchel and a canteen?"

"I believe so, my lord."

Which meant Bertram was on his own, for how long, he did not know. An afternoon? The rest of the damned tour?

He would have to put such notions behind him, and hope—no assume—it would be just one day. Percival probably needed some time to think, and, frankly, he did as well. A walk into Orvieto would help. He would even bring a notebook in the event a muse would compel him to write.

The day was fine, with clear blue skies, warm but not hot. Perfect for a long walk. He finished his breakfast and set out heading east.

Most likely the path was the one Percival took. The marquess never rose early—well, almost never. Had he planned a long journey and needed an early start? Was he trying to avoid Bertram? Perhaps he'd simply gone for a walk and they'd meet on the road.

Probably not. Bertram sighed.

One day apart and already he missed Percival. He missed his genuine enthusiasm for his chosen field of study. He missed his ebullient eagerness to explore life now he was free of past impediments.

Most of all, he missed the warm feeling that stirred within whenever he was alone with the marquess—although he could easily conjure up that sensation while by himself, especially in the morning, still sleep addled and comfortable. Solo sensual release was why he had been delayed to breakfast that morning.

But yesterday morning's sleep-addled contentment was the reason why Percival had been evading him for nearly two days.

Damn Jack to hell. Damn his villainy for breaking an innocent, betraying his trust, and soiling the Atherley name.

No. He would not think about Jack. He would not befoul his holiday with thoughts of the blackguard.

Bertram stopped and looked around. He'd been staring at the ground, for safety's sake, of course, as the dirt path was uneven and unfamiliar. But he'd not been truly conscious of his surroundings. This was the first time he'd ever been to Italy. He might never get a chance again. He should make the most of it.

He clambered up the next hill and sat under a tree. He took out his canteen and drank, taking in the scenery.

All around him was a feast for the senses: sunshine against the lush green of orchards and vineyards, red tile roofs topping houses of golden stone, the sweet song of birds, a whiff of soil and manure in the breeze. And just beyond, Orvieto was poised like a crown on the top of a craggy rock. That Percival had decided to go into town was entirely possible. There was a small museum of Etruscan objects and even shops selling supposed antiquities.

He should go find him.

At Orvieto's rocky base, he followed some people—merchants and tradesmen, he presumed—along a steep path which zigged and zagged higher and higher. At the top was the edge of the hill town, where an omnibus rumbled over the cobblestones before him.

Bertram chuckled. After their first outing to the town, Armand had told him and Percival about the omnibus that took travelers from the valley up to the top. But in this morning's emotional fog, Bertram had managed to forget all about the advice. No matter. The walk had been invigorating.

He wandered the narrow streets aimlessly, hoping but not really expecting to see Percival around every corner. Instead he encountered women chattering to each other while they went about domestic tasks, vendors selling colorful vegetables and fruits, the tantalizing aroma of bakeries. From the main Via del Corso, he turned onto Via del Duomo, continuing down the narrow street until it opened onto a square.

In the middle of the large piazza was the Cathedral, a magnificent sight to behold. The first time he'd seen it, he'd gasped. The sight was still so awe-inspiring, his amazement had not diminished.

The Italian Gothic style was quite different from English Gothic. Instead of dull graying stone, albeit magnificently carved, the Italians went further. The main building was striped, built with alternating courses of black and gray stone. The façade was not merely covered with sculpture, but with colorful mosaics that glittered in the midday sun.

It would be more perfect if Percival were there to share the experience with him.

Bertram took off his straw hat and fanned his face. The cool interior of the Gothic cathedral would offer solace to his weary heart as well as his overheated body.

Inside the vast space clusters of striped stone columns reached all the way up to the vaulted ceiling. Every sound was amplified, including, it seemed, the beating of his lonely heart.

Twenty minutes later and sufficiently refreshed, Bertram escaped the loneliness of the cavernous cathedral for the intimacy of a luncheon at a small café. Yet the fine food and even finer local wine could not fill the emptiness within.

He took another sip of wine to fortify him for the journey back to the villa where, perhaps, Percival would be waiting for him.

Upon arriving at the villa, Bertram handed his hat and canteen to Armand.

"Has the marquess returned?"

"No, my lord." Armand flicked his gaze over Bertram's person with an air of distaste at his dishevelment, the result of a long walk in the hot sun. "Shall I have a bath drawn for you, my lord?"

"No. Thank you." He was too restless for a bath at that moment. "I think I shall take tea in the library, if you don't mind."

A tiny flicker of astonished displeasure marred the valet's otherwise stoic expression. "Very good, my lord."

Before heading off to the library, Bertram offered a grin and a wink as he untied the sleeves of his linen jacket tied around his waist. Taunting Armand playfully was becoming a new pastime.

The villa's library was well-stocked, being that the frequent tenants were academics. Bertram had already ascertained the organization of the grand room was much like a university library. Shelves of art and architectural history, as well as archaeology of all historical eras, seemed to comprise most of the collection. Not surprising, given the clientèle. There was a corner housing volumes of literature. Homer in Greek as well as in English. A few copies of the King James Bible, each with notes on slips of paper. Plus all the usual luminaries of British literature—Chaucer and Shakespeare, Milton and Swift, Byron and Keats, Thackeray and Dickens. Typical for Englishmen abroad.

A maid knocked before entering and setting out his tea. Bertram thanked her and she exited with a curtsy. He took a spot on the floor to examine the lower shelves in the literature corner. He'd not yet had a chance to do so. Given their location, the books were hidden in shadow and their titles obscured.

He pulled out a couple, the spines of which were so worn the gilded letters were unreadable. He flipped open the cover and turned the pages of one of the volumes.

A chill crept up his neck while his cock livened in his trousers. Before him was unabashed pornography, and in Italian no less.

He looked around. The maid had indeed left him quite alone. He grabbed a few more volumes and took them to the library table closer to the light of the windows. He poured his tea and took a few sips to gird his loins, as it were.

The tomes were heavily illustrated adding spice to the text. Besides the Italian—which involved a priest and a nun—there were books in French, Spanish, and Latin. He skimmed the French. A shepherdess looking for a lost sheep found herself in the neighboring pasture and in the arms of a goatherd. The story was accompanied by a lively illustration of said shepherdess with her skirts in disarray as the goatherd guided his long member into what may have been her arsehole. Behind the couple were sheep innocently frolicking amidst grinning goats.

"Armand said you'd be in here."

Bertram slammed the book shut, rattling the tea cup. "Percy." He offered a smile.

Percival briefly raised an eyebrow. "Did you miss me?" He approached.

"Terribly. Where did you go?"

"Back to the Etruscan crypt to make more sketches."

"Even after—"

Percival waved off his reproval. "Yes, yes, even after the unfortunate incident with Belda."

"I'm just surprised. You seemed quite distressed yesterday morning. And I haven't seen you for almost two days." Bertram tried to keep his brooding self-pity at bay.

"You really did miss me, didn't you?"

Apparently his true feelings came through. "Percy, don't seem so surprised. Of course I did. And I worried about your state of mind."

Percival let out a long exhalation. "I did need time to think, to confront my fears." He shook his head. "And I wanted to go back and smooth over any lingering concerns with Belda. Being able to study the crypt is an opportunity not to be missed. I did not want to create any animosity. As a token of good will and of appreciation for Farmer Rossi showing us the tomb, I brought a pot of honey to Mrs. Rossi. Did you know the villa staff make honey here? Mrs. Rossi recognized the emblem on the tag. She said something about it being from the senior's house."

"*Casa da signore?*"

"Yes, that's it. That's what she said."

"The gentleman's house. This house." Bertram smiled. "And what you did was rather courageous, even if it did not entail much risk."

Percival moved closer to the library table. "I owe you an apology for avoiding you."

"Percy…" Bertram knew any confession would be difficult. He really just wanted Percival to be with him.

"No, Bertie, listen. Confronting you was my true fear." He drew in a breath and let it out slowly. "Because then I'd have to think about Jack."

"Jesus, Percy, I don't want you to think of Jack every time we're together."

"I don't want to either."

For one moment, their gazes met, unspoken emotion conveyed in one pained look.

Percival broke the spell when he rounded the library table. "What are you reading?"

Bertram's cheeks burned as his hand shrouded the cover. "Nothing as exciting as sketching an Etruscan tomb, I'm sure."

"Oh?" Percival slid the book out from Bertram's flattened palm. He opened to a random page and was greeted with an image of a scantily dressed young woman sucking the cock of an elderly gentleman while a young man wearing a vicar's collar stood behind her and aimed his erect, and overly large, prick between her thighs.

Heat crept across Bertram's scalp as his own cock grew to match the size of the vicar's. "I'm certain it is a metaphor," he said with a rasp. "And I apologize if such a book offends you."

Percival gaped momentarily before expelling a guffaw. "I'm not an innocent." He clasped Bertram's hand briefly. "But this is rather ridiculous."

"Well, perhaps because it involves a vicar."

"That's what's ridiculous?" Percival's brows shot up.

"I don't doubt some women participate in situations like these."

Percival sobered. "You're right, of course. But I have no knowledge of such situations involving women."

"Nor do I. Just men."

"Oh?"

Damn. Had he just revealed too much about himself?

"Where?" Percival asked.

"Cambridge."

"Ah." A simple response. No implications that Oxford was any different. "Involving you?"

Double damn. "I may have been involved in situations similar to this. What about you?"

"Me?" Percival blushed.

"At Oxford."

"Utterly abstemious. I led a life more monkish than a monk." He pointed at the vicar in the image. "Definitely more monkish than this fellow." As Percival studied the illustration, his blush deepened. "So you would simply suck a man's cock?"

"Or he would suck mine. It really didn't matter."

Percival's brow knitted in something akin to horror. "Did you fancy any of these fellows?"

"You mean were we sweethearts?"

"Well, yes."

Bertram sighed. "Some trysts lasted longer than others."

"Do you ever think you broke another man's heart?"

"Only as much as mine got broken."

Percival's eyes widened as if in utter shock. "That is a rather…cavalier attitude to…to such an act." The last was said with a touch of disgust.

"We were only having a bit of fun—" *Damn.* Realization flooded over Bertram. "Oh, God, Percy, I apologize. Sometimes I imagine you led a different life than what you did."

Silence hung in the air. "Jack made me do it to him. And he was rough."

Damn, damn, damn, and double damn. "Percy, please, you don't need to—"

"I think I do, Bertie." Percival blew out a breath. "He only did it to me once. I suppose to teach me how to…service him."

"Jesus Christ," Bertram muttered, his gut churning at the sheer horror.

Percival grabbed his hand, squeezing it, then letting go. "I recall liking it, though. What little I remember." A faraway look haunted his eyes.

A flash of a fantasy where he reminded Percival what fellatio felt like flitted in Bertram's mind. Where he introduced Percival to the sensations one could have while relaxed and enjoying the act. Not mere physical response to an act performed by a villain with ill intent. "Percy, I'm so sorry I dredged up that memory."

"I'm the one who should apologize." Percival once again grasped Bertram's hand on the library table. "Being with you has been confusing at times. My only experience has been with…" His hesitation spoke volumes. "Someone else. And, after a brief honeymoon, the experiences were not altogether pleasant. So when I feel," he looked askance and cleared his throat, "desire for you, there is a tiny bit of, well, revulsion." He met Bertram's gaze, probably finding the utter shock he felt reflected there. "Not for you. I don't mean for you. I mean it's so ingrained in my body's physical reaction that when I get aroused I feel apprehension."

"I understand." He was trying to at least, each and every day. "Thank you for explaining it that way."

Percival cleared his throat. "And since Cambridge? How have you satisfied yourself over the years?"

With fantasies of you. "Mostly by my own hand."

Percival blushed. "Do you miss it?"

"Miss what?"

"Sucking a cock, or having yours sucked, as you so blithely put it."

Bertram chuckled. "Of course I do. I will admit that openly. But those carefree days are over. I hope to forge a deeper sort of intimacy and connection at this stage of my life."

Percival's renewed blush was accompanied by a beaming smile. "I, as well."

So, there *was* hope.

"Well," said Percival as he sat his dusty satchel on the floor. "I shall take my leave. I would like a bath before dinner. Then tonight I shall review and rewrite today's notes." He placed his hand over Bertram's on the desk. "I'm going back tomorrow to the Etruscan crypt. I'd love your company."

"I fear I would only be in your way."

"I disagree. I think you would be an inspiration." Percival smiled. "I'll see you at dinner?" It was said with hopefulness and not assumption.

"Yes. Absolutely." He'd take any damn second to be with the marquess that he could.

PERCIVAL CURLED ON his side hugging a pillow, trying to fall asleep. While his body was exhausted, his thoughts were running a non-stop race, taunting him with possibilities involving Bertram.

He supposed the seed to his overgrowth of thoughts had been laid at dinner, he sitting at the head of the table, Bertram at his side. They'd had an amiable meal devoid of any talk about past unpleasantness, only about future possibilities. Well, mostly about Percival's plans to sketch and document the Etruscan catacomb. But Bertram had said he was hoping to soak up the ambiance of Italy and France to incorporate into his stories.

Dinner had an air of ambition and aspiration. Unlike the last day and a half which had been stultifying and depressing.

Waking from a nightmare of Jack and discovering Bertie had filled him with confusion. His stomach had churned from the memory of Jack, while his prick had stirred with the promise of Bertram.

And a day without Bertram had filled him with acute longing. A day away from Jack had always filled him with relief followed by dread for the next time he'd see him.

Tonight at dinner had been relaxing, perhaps because of the wine, definitely because of Bertram's casual attitude and gracious attentiveness.

Afterward, they'd gone to the library. More wine—*vin santo*, a lovely, locally made amber-colored sweet wine with a hint of chestnut—and the recollection of the book Bertram had been perusing earlier lulled Percival into a state of tranquility. While the book had been tucked away on a shelf, pictures of fellatio had danced in Percival's head, then continued thrilling him in bed. Specifically images of Bertram sucking his cock.

And Percival utterly enjoying the act with abandon.

Until his mind dredged up feelings of shame, and he grabbed a pillow in consolation, his nightshirt binding his legs as he pulled them up.

Would he ever be able to divorce the idea of sexual pleasure from his past emotional anguish?

He had to. If he and Bertram were ever going to form a more profound relationship, he simply had to.

Percival would have to make a concerted effort to suppress any memories that got in the way of enjoying a sensual relationship with Bertram. Perhaps they could start by being face to face. During the day time. Or at night with lamps blazing.

Or just by being together.

He knew his Bertie, knew what he sounded like, what he smelled like, how he moved.

Percival would know it was Bertram touching him, holding him. He would. Right?

There was only one way to find out.

Bertram stared up at the night-blackened ceiling in his bedroom. Percival's revelation earlier that day had plagued him, had subdued him so much he had spent most of dinner listening and not engaging in lively discussion as he usually did.

Over after-dinner *vin santo* in the library, Percival had reiterated his invitation to join him at the Etruscan tomb. Spending the day with Percival would be a joy to his heart, but torture to his cock.

But continence was the challenge when one was in love with a damaged soul.

Love. Was that what it was? Well, if not love then something equally demanding to one's heart and psyche.

Lust?

Surely not so base an impulse.

Percival made him feel serene, at ease with the world, yet at the same time stirred his libidinous senses to a frenzy. A frenzy that roused once again now that he lay in the dark contemplating the blond marquess.

Bertram slipped his hand under the covers and grabbed his eager cock, groaning as relief washed over him.

He didn't need to be on top. He'd be happy on his knees sucking Percival's cock. But, oh God, if Percival were on his bed, his legs spread wide enough for Bertram to slip inside… Bertram balancing over him on stretched arms… those plump lips and blue eyes setting off a face twisted in erotic oblivion while he slowly pumped the exquisitely tight arsehole—

A knock on the bedroom door stopped him cold.

Bertram got up and grabbed his dressing gown, not putting it on, just holding it over his erection.

"Yes?" he said through the door.

"Bertie? May I come in?"

Despite the plaintive urgency of the request, Percival's voice revived Bertram's unslaked cock to its previous state during his still-fresh fantasy.

He opened the door. In the glow of the lamp he carried, Percival's gaze swept over Bertram's body, his eyes widening when he returned to regard Bertram's face.

"I wanted to be with you. But now I just feel awkward."

"Because I sleep in the nude?"

"I admit I did not expect to be greeted by a naked man. One never does, I suppose."

Bertram chuckled as he waved Percival inside. "I was awake anyway." Still holding his bunched-up robe over his crotch, he closed the door.

Percival shifted on his feet, his grip tight on the lamp. "I've been thinking about the other night at the farmhouse. I would like to… sleep with you like that again."

Bertram's cock responded favorably. He tightened his hold on the robe. "I would like that, as well."

"Oh, grand," Percival said with a breathy exhale. He set the lamp on the dressing table and snuffed out the flame, leaving only the dull glow of moonlight through sheer curtains. "I was so afraid of your reaction."

"Percy, please don't ever be afraid of me."

"But of course I'm frightened, Bertie. Jack was my first and my last. I have no idea how two men may interact together other than what he did to me."

"I think you and I have been interacting quite agreeably so far."

Percival's beaming smile set his heart to pounding.

"You know you don't have to keep holding your robe like that."

"Promise you won't be afraid of what lurks beneath?"

"Promise." Percival licked his lips.

Bertram stripped the robe away and tossed it on the slipper chair. The night air cooled his ardor for a fleeting moment before his erection stirred anew.

A sharp gasp escaped Percival's lips.

"That impressive, eh?"

"I don't really know. My fantasies were never very specific."

"But you have had fantasies of me."

Percival glanced aside. "I have. Mostly that we're holding each other and it's safe and warm."

A twinge of pathos gripped Bertram's heart. "Shall I wear a nightshirt?"

"Do you even own one?"

"You know I do. I couldn't very well sleep stripped to the buff on the train." Bertram laughed. "Armand lays one out for me every night despite its being untouched and draped in the very same place in the morning."

Silence lasting a beat too long gave Bertram his answer. He grabbed the nightshirt from the foot of the bed and hustled into it.

Percival shed his dressing gown and laid it on the slipper chair. Bertram held out his hand and Percival took it, entwining his fingers and squeezing during the few steps to the bed.

They climbed in. Percival settled into the arc of Bertram's body, the curve of his bum nestled against Bertram's hips.

His cock responded immediately, the now-hard shaft prodding and seeking the cleft, the generous cut of the nightshirt not offering any restraint.

Bertram jumped from the bed.

"Bertie?" Percival's soft plea was edged with concern.

"Sorry." Bertram fumbled in the dark, searching for more clothes. "I should wear drawers. Your... your—" *glorious body* "presence is—" *maddeningly arousing* "very distracting."

The susurration of sheets signaled Percival had sat up. "Come back to bed. Please. I understand this must be an unusual request, especially for a man of your experience, but I need to feel you at my side. I need to feel your arousal and know you will not take advantage. I should take comfort when your potency presses against me and you do not force me to comply with your physical needs." Percival drew in a long breath before letting out a tremulous exhale.

Bertram slipped back under the covers, this time pulling the nightshirt snugly around his hips and thighs. Percival stretched himself catlike against him. Bertram gingerly wrapped his arms around Percival's upper body, being careful not to stray anywhere near his crotch.

Percival sighed as he nestled more deeply into Bertram's embrace, maneuvering his buttocks until Bertram's cock, even restrained as it was by the nightshirt, lay in the cleft.

Bertram pressed his cheek to Percival's shoulder and closed his eyes, wishing for sleep to descend swiftly. If burning for his Percy was the price he had to pay in order to win his trust, then so be it.

"I like that," Percival purred.

Bertram froze in mortification. He'd been absently brushing Percival's soft skin with his lips, not daring to kiss, just gently stroking back and forth.

"Why did you stop?"

"Percy, I apologize. It was inadvertent. I don't mean to seem the seducer."

Percival turned in his arms until their breaths mingled in the night. "I liked it. It was tender." He slid a finger along Bertram's jaw. "I'm not used to such tenderness."

Bertram's heart ached at the confession, then began pounding as Percival moved his face closer until he pecked a delicate kiss on Bertram's astonished mouth.

Every pore flared, as desire tingled across his flesh.

Percival pressed on, kissing with more vigor, more intention, until their tongues twined in an erotic tangle. He slithered on top, straddling Bertram, their shafts pressing together through thin cloth.

With a deep growl, Percival rolled off to curl at Bertram's side.

"Hold me."

Bertram complied, keeping his arms above the waist.

Percival rubbed his bum against Bertram's waning erection, sparking it to life. "Whatever will the servants think if they find us in bed together?"

"Let's hope they assume our female bedmates fled before dawn."

Percival chuckled. "Or that we're corrupt aristocrats."

Bertram kissed Percival's head. "Sweet dreams, Percy."

Little by little, Percival's muscles eased, relaxing into Bertram's embrace. A minute later came the even breathing of sleep.

His Percy was discovering trust. Perhaps the nightmares of the past would be overtaken by pleasing memories and be forgotten.

CHAPTER TEN

One delight in being a trusted first mate was sharing with the
captain his special reserve of Madeira wine.
— *The Adventures of Paolo the Pirate Hunter*

Rather than being in Percival's way while he worked at the
Etruscan tomb, Bertram discovered he was a valuable asset.

First, the villa's horse and cart were not available that
morning so the two had to carry all their supplies strapped to their
backs. Besides luncheon and canteens of water, there was quite a
bit of equipment needed for the survey. Lamps to light dark
corners, soft brushes for clearing debris off sculpted rock, a tape
measure and a folding ruler, two different types of compasses—
one for drawing circles, one for determining direction—pencils
and notebooks, a set of watercolors, folding camp chairs, and an
easel.

"I do wish we had a camera," Percival said as they trudged
along. "Although I suppose it is simply too dark in the catacomb.
And any smoke or flares would damage the murals."

He chuckled when he caught Bertram's confused glance. "A few of the students at Oxford have been experimenting with photography. Burning magnesium wire can illuminate a darkened room for practically a whole minute with a flame as intense as the sun." He snorted. "It's all rather dangerous."

"Our lanterns will have to suffice."

Then, once inside the tomb, Percival directed Bertram in all manner of archaeological preparation. Wearing a cloth over his nose and mouth so he did not breathe in too much dust, Bertram gently brushed and swept the columns and the benches revealing a crispness to the carvings. Percival set up lamps and his easel to sketch the murals.

When he finished his task, Bertram stepped outside into the suddenly bright sun and quaffed water from his canteen, the heat of midday portending what the next several hours would be like. They would be there all day, Percival had warned him, and would walk back in the cooler early evening.

"Bertie!"

Alarm goaded Bertram to rush back inside. Percival stood in the middle of the mural room, turning slowly as he surveyed the space, the flicker of lamplight dancing shadows around him.

"Eureka! I've got it!"

Bertram went to his side and Percival grabbed his hand, a thrill bolting up his arm to quicken his heart.

"And what is it that you've discovered?"

"My first instincts were correct. I'm sure of it. See, there are two separate spaces." He motioned to the foyer. "One for the living." He spread his arms wide. "And one for the dead. Each room a place to celebrate life." He blinked and let out a long satisfied sigh, then grabbed Bertram by the shoulders and pulled him in for a kiss.

The thrill shot right to his crotch. Bertram kissed him back with enthusiasm.

Percival broke free, blushing and smiling. "I like that. I like kissing."

"I'm available whenever you want to do just that."

The marquess pecked his lips. "I would love to neck with you in the coolness of this ancient ruin, but I really need you to take notes for me while I think out loud."

Bertram chuckled at the directive. "I will do so gladly." He winked. "We'll continue the other course of action later."

Despite the sensual possibilities, Percival proceeded undaunted. He handed Bertram a leather-bound notebook and a gold propelling pencil topped with a yellow gemstone.

"The decorations painted on the benches depicted in the murals match the decorations carved into the benches in the entryway. So the two spaces must be connected. The people in the mural are reclining and drinking wine as if in a symposium—"

"A meeting?"

"No. Well, I mean, only sort of. A symposium was an ancient Greek party where men drank and discussed philosophy." Percival went to one part of the mural and pointed. "But here we also have women. So the Etruscans seemed to allow women in such events. And because of that detail, I thought perhaps this was meant to be a familial celebration." He grinned. "Hence I concluded that the living family was meant to commune with the deceased, each in their separate spaces."

Bertram took notes as well as he could. Percival's confidence and poise were utterly beguiling.

Percival pointed to one couple. "Here we have two men holding hands." He turned and pointed to the opposite wall. "And here, two women holding hands. This points to deep affiliations. Friendship, family—"

"Lovers."

Percival stared at Bertram. "I hadn't thought about that. Are there women like us?"

"I'm certain of it." He'd only heard of such women. He'd never actually met one. He resumed scribbling in the notebook.

"Lovers of all sorts." Percival nodded as he slowly surveyed the space once again. "It's like an *agape* feast."

Bertram looked up. "*Agape*? Isn't that a Greek word for love?"

"Yes, a sort of higher love, for one's god or affection for humanity."

"As opposed to *eros*—passionate, physical love."

Percival blushed. "There are many words for love, if you remember your Greek. Such as *philia*."

Bertram grinned. "The love between friends."

Another blush. "Early Christians would celebrate a funerary feast in the catacombs that was much like their Eucharistic *agape* feasts. The Romans before them not only had funerary feasts but commemorative banquets at family cemeteries. Perhaps the Etruscans similarly used their underground sepulchers not as places of grief and mourning, but as places of celebration."

Bertram eyed the farmer's cups hanging on the wall by the entrance. "An enduring Italian tradition."

Percival chuckled. "And it is so cool down here during the hot summer, and probably warmer during the cold winter. The deceased are inviting the family to continue to share meals with them even in death." He spun around. "Look at all of this. It's incredible. And I can't imagine such an incredible space went to waste as a mere tomb."

"But plenty of tombs are merely monuments to the dead, aren't they? Surely the Egyptian pyramids have no other use than as mausoleums."

"I suppose. But there is something to be said about an enduring local tradition." With a satisfied smile, Percival wrapped his arm around Bertram's shoulder. "I think there is evidence for this catacomb as a sort of dining room. I'll write up the notes with drawings and compile a report for Professor Bellamy."

Bertram clasped Percival's hand draped on his shoulder. Percival leaned his head against him.

"Thank you for being here with me. Thank you for listening and helping me."

Bertram kissed the top of Percival's head. "I will be here for you as long as you need."

Percival gave his hand a squeezed then unwrapped his arm. "Will you share my bed with me tonight?"

A joyous warmth crept along Bertram's flesh. "I will. Gladly."

Too bad it was only luncheon and bedtime was so very far away.

A week or so later

PERCIVAL LOOKED UP from his notebook to gaze out the library window at the indigo sky. Despite the late hour, twilight still lingered. His endeavors over the last few days had teased his brain into a frenzy of thought. Could there really be a tradition of the living celebrating alongside the dead? Did this have anything to do with similar celebrations centuries later? Did one culture simply adopt and adapt the practices and customs of the one before it? Such as what the Etruscans did with the Greeks? Did the symposium metamorphose into the Christian Eucharistic feast?

As he re-wrote his notes from that day, he reviewed his sketches and watercolors, noting where he needed more data or needed to get a closer look. On the other side of the room Bertram sat at a writing desk scribbling away, sometimes smiling and chuckling to himself, then leaning back in his chair and sipping vin santo with a look of accomplishment.

He sipped from his own glass of vin santo. The tawny liquor's taste of figs and honey would forever remind him of this blissful time with Bertram.

Percival could get used to such a life. Spending the day with his best friend, then the evening as well, each occupied with their own pursuits and thoughts.

Then retreating to the same bed.

Well, that had only happened twice. It was his own damn fault really. Bertram was more than willing, but Percival kept thinking the servants would grow suspicious. He did not want to give Professor Bellamy a bad reputation by association because of his indiscretions. And he did not want the professor to think he might be something other than a conventional Englishman. Professor Bellamy would be returning to the villa in a few weeks and did not need unnecessary aggravation.

Still, ever since that first night he and Bertram had spent in each other's arms, now over a week ago, they'd shared some furtive kisses, some hand holding, some hugs.

But maybe, someday, they would be able to spend every night together without a thought for the consequences.

"Percy?" Bertram's query broke his thoughts.

"Yes?"

"What sort of things might one find in an Etruscan tomb if one discovered one in pristine condition? A tomb that no one else had ever found before?"

"Besides funerary urns and sarcophagi?"

"Yes."

Percival thought for a moment. "Lots of Greek pottery, I suppose. Greek colonists and merchants traded with the Etruscans."

"What about gold and jewels?"

A moment's realization set Percival to laughing. "Are your pirates planning on raiding a catacomb?"

Bertram grinned. "And Paolo brings them to justice, giving the local museum all of the artifacts."

"What a magnificent story." Percival continued to chuckle. "Yes, the Etruscans are known for their finely wrought gold work. I suppose one would find a body if one opened a sarcophagus. Perhaps wearing jewelry."

"Or a family of bodies, if it were a family tomb."

"And don't forget that modern Italian peasants probably already know about the crypt—"

"And the pirate kidnaps them. That's how he finds out about the tomb." Bertram bent his head and began writing furiously.

A smile curled Percival's lips. While he had been visiting the catacomb every day, Bertram had only sometimes joined him. Other times Bertram had been venturing out on his own, hiking and exploring, always with his journal.

Apparently he had been coming up with some fantastical stories.

Percival resumed his study of his own notes. The Etruscans surely celebrated their dead, celebrated the life lived, and continued to celebrate it after death. "We English have it all wrong," he said aloud, "with our mourning black draped on our persons and in our parlors, our depressing dirges, our dreary corteges. We should have joyful celebrations of someone's life after their death."

"Or," offered Bertram, "celebrate the fact that they are now dead and life can go on."

Percival stared at Bertram as a chilling shudder shook him.

"Blast," Bertram muttered. "Percy, I didn't mean—"

"You did, though. And you're right." He sighed. "Sometimes death means others can live."

"Which is a reason to celebrate."

The sentiment brought warmth and a smile back to him. He sipped his wine.

"Percy?"

"I'm all right, Bertie." Especially knowing the viscount cared so much for his well-being.

"Good." Bertram's smile held a hint of relief. He bent over his notebook and continued to scribble.

Percival swallowed the last of his wine. Yes, he could get very used to such a life.

Unfortunately, they would have to depart soon for France and meet Father's connections.

Too soon.

CHAPTER ELEVEN

"Every port of call, my dear Barnaby, holds its own charms. And aversions."
— *The Adventures of Paolo the Pirate Hunter*

Nice, France

Bertram gazed out the carriage window as the wheels climbed a low incline toward their next place of respite, a villa overlooking the city of Nice. In the distance, the Mediterranean, or, rather, the *Baie des Anges*, the Bay of Angels, gleamed a most unearthly shade of blue—azure with hints of turquoise and lapis. A gentle breeze through the open windows helped ease the warmth of the afternoon sun.

Beside him Percival stared at the same view, his countenance impassive, his emotions indecipherable. The mere fact the marquess was not impressed with the glorious vista meant something weighed heavily on his mind.

Bertram squeezed Percival's hand. "Are you well, my lord?"

Percival sulked. "I am, my lord viscount."

Bertram chuckled.

An exhalation sent Percival leaning back into his own corner. "I miss Italy."

"We can return once you've performed your familial obligations."

The suggestion elicited a muffled whimper.

Their last days in Italy had been spent with Percival finally capitulating to his aristocratic duty and writing letters to his father's contacts. While Percival had sighed heavily and muttered indistinctly throughout his correspondence, Bertram had continued to write and edit. He amused himself with the notion of Paolo the Pirate Hunter attacking some disagreeable task with lamentations rather than force of wit and courage, then thought better of it.

After that apparently onerous business was complete, Percival had commenced handling his own affairs. He made two copies of his report on the Etruscan tomb, one to leave in the library at the villa, one to keep for himself. He posted a letter to Professor Bellamy with a summary of his findings, letting him know the full report was available at the villa, and providing him with the address of the villa in France. Once finished, Percival had announced he felt ready to continue on their journey.

Although now it seemed he was having misgivings.

"We can search for Visigothic ruins next time we're in Italy," Bertram offered in consolation.

That brought a smile to Percival's face. "I think we might find some here." He gestured at the view beyond the window.

Percival had insisted they travel via rail from Umbria to Nice so they could experience the landscape. The countryside was spectacular, with mountains higher than anything Bertram had ever imagined, and positively mesmerizing views of the Mediterranean coast. The route they traveled was purportedly the one traveled by the Visigoths when they kidnapped the Roman princess Galla Placidia and took her to Spain during the fifth century.

"A boat might have been quicker," Bertram had commented at the time. "What with all the treacherous mountains."

"The Visigoths attacked Italy from the north," Percival had explained. "They were not seafarers. They were used to traveling over mountains."

The carriage slowed as they arrived at the villa, the gravel drive golden with the reflected light of the Mediterranean. The edifice seemed of an older time, perhaps built over a century ago, with two stories and a third hidden behind the generous roof. The entrance on the ground floor was embraced by ganged pilasters which continued up to the first floor where they were surmounted by a handsome pediment. Agave and citrus trees grew in abundance along the foundation, while further along the drive, palms waved in the breeze. Bertram had never before seen such an exotic and magical sight.

At the base of the stone steps leading to the front entrance, servants lined up to greet them upon their arrival. Armand had timed the event rather perfectly, or the staff had waited patiently. Bertram was quite unused to such efforts, but he knew his betters did such ceremonies.

The footmen opened the carriage door and Percival descended first. Bertram fell in behind, ready to follow the marquess's lead.

Armand was already there, having done the sensible thing by traveling via steamship. Bertram had assured the fastidious valet that he would personally look after the proper grooming of the marquess on the rail journey. Armand had thought about that for only a moment before deciding setting up the house in Nice was far more important than whether Percival shaved or not.

Speaking in French, Armand introduced the three servants. Madame Frossard was the cook, a dour woman about Bertram's age and quite pregnant. Her hair was wrapped in a faded scarf, a chain with a severe silver cross hung around her neck. Her husband, Monsieur Frossard, was the man-of-all-work. He was much older than she, with a touch of gray in his beard. Blandine, a girl perhaps still in her teens, was Madame's sister and the household's girl-of-all-work. The trio came with the house rental, and Armand apologized to Percival—in English—that the staff was so inadequate.

Blushes and wide eyes suggested Blandine was somewhat enchanted by Percival. Of course, who would not be taken by the dashing marquess?

She curtsied when he stood before her. "*Bienvenue, monsieur le marquis,*" she said in welcome.

Madame shot the girl a disproving look.

As they entered the villa, Percival just smiled his usual dazzling smile, surely unaware of any effect he was having on the girl.

"My lord," Armand said in English, "I will show you to your rooms now."

He indicated the staircase to the right with an intricate wrought-iron handrail. The stairs of an ancient, golden stone shone where the footfalls of so many before had trodden. They proceeded to the first floor and gathered on the landing.

"The views are magnificent from the drawing room on the first floor, but even more so from the bedrooms," Armand said.

They climbed the stairs one more turn and arrived at the bedroom level with several doorways along the corridor, some of which had wooden plaques over the doors with a line of text in white letters and dainty painted decorations.

"There are multiple suites as you can see." Armand gestured to all the doors. "But the best one is the master's suite, on the south-facing side. It is large, with two bedrooms, each with fairly modern baths. You will see the views are quite spectacular." He exhibited an uncharacteristic enthusiasm.

As Armand toyed with the ring of keys, trying each in the lock, Bertram got a better look at the plaque over the door. Delicate yellow and white flowers surrounded elegant script, each with an attribution in smaller letters. He looked more closely at the plaque above one of the guest bedrooms. A quote from the Bible.

La charité est patiente, elle est douce. La charité n'est point envieuse ~ 1 Corinthiens 13:4.

Charity is patient, is kind, is not envious. A quote from the first letter of Paul to the Corinthians in the New Testament.

Above another guest bedroom was *La charité n'est point ambitieuse; elle ne cherche point ses propres intérêts ~ 1 Corinthiens 13:5.*

Charity is not ambitious, does not seek her own interests.

What did it all mean?

"Here we go." Armand opened the door to the suite.

Bertram looked over the doorway. *La foi, l'espérance, et la charité ~ la plus grande des trois, c'est la charité ~ 1 Corinthiens 13:13.*

Of faith, hope, and charity, the greatest of these is charity.

Percival nudged him. "Bible quotes about charity? In a rented villa? Rather brazen of someone, no?"

Bertram laughed. "Perhaps the servants have a sense of humor."

As they entered the space Bertram instantly understood Armand's earlier enthusiasm.

The second floor suite was, from an outside observer, tucked behind the garret outlined by the roof. And, yet, through the doors to a balcony, the suite overlooked the town of Nice spilling down the hill out to the sea, a few scattered palm trees framing the fabulous prospect.

Armand stood beaming, momentarily lost in thought as he took in the view. Suddenly, he shook his head. "Pardon me, my lord," he said to Percival.

"Don't concern yourself." Percival placed a hand on Armand's shoulder. "It is, as you say, quite a spectacular view."

"Thank you, my lord." The valet seemed rather affected by something. Perhaps because he was a Frenchman returned to France. He cleared his throat. "My lord Norrington's room is here on the left," he said with an elegant presentational gesture.

"Viscount Ravensburgh's room on the right." He nodded to Bertram. "I took the liberty of unpacking your trunks."

"Thank you."

"Very good, my lord. Luncheon will be served in the dining room in one hour. If there is nothing else, I will take my leave."

Percival smiled. "Thank you, Armand. You are indispensable."

Bertram went to the window to take in the view. Beyond Nice, the Mediterranean glittered like a sapphire. Percival sidled up alongside, clasping his hand.

"We seem to be miles away from the sea," commented Bertram.

"It's only one mile, and quite walkable I am told, along a lovely boulevard." Percival squeezed Bertram's hand. "It is customary to stay in a grand hotel closer to the sea front, but Armand thought we would have a bit more privacy tucked away on a hill."

"Far from the madding crowd?"

Percival chuckled. "I suppose. You do have to admit the view is beautiful."

"It is." Bertram grinned. "So you are willing to give France a chance?"

"Yes." Percival squeezed his hand. "Especially since we have our very own suite of rooms."

"No sneaking down a corridor late at night trying to avoid the servants."

Percival leaned his head on Bertram's shoulder. The marquess was going to be just fine in France.

PERCIVAL PLACED HIS morning post on the terrace table and set down his coffee cup. He pulled out the delightfully provincial wicker-work chair and sat.

He drew in a long inhalation. Breakfasting on the terrace was absolutely exquisite with just a hint of a sea breeze off the Mediterranean.

Oh, and that view.

Percival smiled as he sipped his coffee and took in the vista.

The still of the morning was shattered by Bertram passing noisily through the drawing room's terrace doors. He emitted a mewling sigh as he sat in the chair on the other side of the micro-mosaic inlaid table.

"Oh, I slept very well," he pronounced, *à propos* of nothing. "Too many nights on a train made me forget what a proper bed could feel like."

Percival glared. "Good morning. There's coffee. It's quite good."

A teasing smirk played upon Bertram's luscious lips. "Thank you." He raised a brow. "My lord."

Percival scoffed as the viscount chuckled and poured his coffee from the silver coffee pot. A scoot of his chair and his view now included his terrace mate. The exquisite vista just got a little bit better.

"Armand sorted through the post that's been accumulating," he said. "Yours are on the tray on the console table just inside." He waved at the opened French doors.

Bertram retrieved his mail then sat, sorting through the envelopes. "Oh, good. Mama has written." He chuckled. "She must miss me." He drank his coffee as he examined one envelope in particular. "And Nicholas! How wonderful."

"What does he say? If you don't mind telling me, that is. I only received a series of postcards from him, one of which was pictorial highlights of Cambridge presumably to taunt me for my academic choices."

Bertram chuckled as he put down his cup and gently opened the envelope. He scanned the contents of the letter. "The London doctor he's been working for is becoming increasingly eccentric, but he's muddling on. He's nursing a broken heart and hopes my—" Bertram broke off and folded the letter.

"Hopes what?"

"Hopes I am doing well," Bertram murmured before taking a sip of coffee.

That did not quite sound right. "Does he mention me?"

Bertram's cup clinked too loudly against the saucer. "Percy, Nicky does not know we are together."

"But he knows you're staying with me at this villa, correct?" Percival pointed to the letter.

"No. My mother forwarded the letter. It was sent to the St. Albans cottage."

"Oh." Percival toyed with the handle of his coffee cup. "Is there a reason?"

"Last I saw him, when Uncle Robert was dying, I told him I was enamored with someone. I didn't specify whom. There was so much Nicky had to deal with at that moment. To tell him his cousin was attracted to his brother's former lover seemed too much to reveal."

Percival's heart pounded. "Enamored of me?"

Bertram smiled through his blush. "I think you know that already."

"Well, yes, but, I mean, I didn't think—" *Damn*, he was suddenly nervous. "I just never realized you've, um, felt this way," he gestured between them, "since before we embarked on our journey."

The smile widened. "Since well before we embarked on our journey."

"You've never said anything."

"I think I've shown you how I feel."

"I like hearing the words."

Bertram chortled. "I am quite enamored of you, Percival Wood." He reached along the mosaic table top and squeezed Percival's hand.

A flush crept up the back of Percival's neck to heat his face as joy made him grin. If only every moment could be filled with such luscious emotion.

The clink of porcelain on a metal tray preceded the entrance of the maid—the young one—carrying a tray with rolls and coffee.

The reverie was broken.

"*Bonjour, monsieur le marquis*," she said as she curtsied with the tray. "*Le café est frais et trop bon.*" She licked her lower lip as she held his gaze.

Fresh and good? Good God. Had she just insinuated the coffee was primed for a tryst? "*Merci.*" Conveying polite gratitude was all he could muster. Percival maintained an impassive demeanor so as not to incite the passions of the poor girl.

She remained unmoving until Bertram moved the plate of rolls and pot of coffee from the tray to the table.

"*Merci, Blandine,*" the viscount said with a hint of annoyance.

The blushing and flustered maid quickly grabbed the empty coffee pot, curtsied again, and left hurriedly.

Bertram chuckled as Percival let out a sigh of exasperation.

"I hope I don't find her in my bed," he muttered. "I wouldn't know what to do."

"What's this?" Bertram frowned as he pulled a map out from under the plate of rolls. "Percy, this is not a map of Nice, you know. Or anywhere in France."

"No, it is not. Rather it is a map of London." He glanced at the legend. "Belgravia, in fact."

"London? We've just traveled thousands of miles and you're thinking about returning already?"

"Now I am free to live as I choose and unguarded, I would like to move to London. These are lists of houses for lease," Percival tapped a stack of pages, "and these are maps of their locations. My agent is astoundingly organized. He's numbered everything, see." He pointed to the map and its corresponding descriptive sheet.

"I do see." Bertram perused one of the lists.

"He'll be sending me these packets while we are abroad. Father insisted I do something productive while I am away."

"Hmm." Bertram compared the listings to the map. "As opposed to doing research for an Oxford professor?"

Percival laughed. "Father means I should plan for my future as he imagines it should be. As the son of a duke. I'm really looking for a private getaway in town. Nothing grand. I don't plan on holding lavish balls."

Bertram snorted. He placed a sheet on the table and pointed to the description. "Four bedrooms, my lord? Whatever will you do with four bedrooms?"

Percival snatched the listing away. "My agent is simply providing me with available houses without judgment. I'll have you know there are listings with a mere two bedrooms among these." He swept his hand over the table. "I haven't quite decided what sort of lifestyle I might want to maintain. Perhaps I'll wish to entertain visitors a great deal. I'll need loads of bedrooms for that. Possibly even more than four."

"I see. I suppose a future duke must project at least a façade of extravagance."

Percival scowled. "By the way, we have an invitation to a dinner party tonight."

"Already? We've only just arrived."

"Apparently the English expatriates are so bored here anyone new is the talk of the town. I would like for us to go."

"Do you know any of these people?"

"Not a bleeding soul. They know my parents, or my father, rather. He was popular in his youth, it seems."

"All right. I hope what I have packed will be appropriate for such esteemed friends."

"Never fear. Armand will make an assessment of your wardrobe." Percival gazed out at the view again. "After breakfast, let's explore this little city."

"Absolutely." Bertram chuckled. "We can buy postcards of Nice and taunt Nicky with our adventures."

"You would tell him?"

"He'll discover my whereabouts soon enough. Especially when I write to him from your rented villa."

"Quite." Percival beamed. "And we must walk along the *Promenade des Anglais*. After all, we are English."

"And already well-known for that attribute by some of the residents."

Percival took a swallow of coffee. He dreaded whatever was to happen that night. But in the meantime, he would spend the day with someone who was enamored of him.

His heart skipped a beat. *Enamored.*

BERTRAM'S EVENING ATTIRE was utterly appropriate for the casual affair held at the home of Basil Goring, the Earl of Berrick. His summer linen suit was neither severe nor shabby. Percival in his black tail coat, however, might have been a bit overdressed.

"We only ask our guests to dress as if they are going down for dinner," said Lord Berrick as he shook their hands upon entering the drawing room at the opulent flat. "Where they might imagine that dinner to be is entirely up to them."

Apparently not just a few of the guests imagined that dinner to be at a beach in the middle of the day. And they lounged upon the furniture as if they were enjoying the sunshine on the shore.

The spectacle was enlivening and amusing. And not too unexpected as the earl did live along the vibrant *Promenade des Anglais.*

"I fear I am overdressed," Percival murmured in Bertram's ear.

"Not at all, my dear marquess," he confided quietly. "Just say you have dressed as if you were dining with the queen. Which you might do one of these days. Especially once you are ensconced in London."

Percival glowered, then chuckled with a shake of his head.

The lanky, graying earl called over a manservant with a tray of champagne-filled coupes. "Please," he said to Percival and Bertram, "indulge." He turned to Percival. "And I want to hear all about you, Percival Wood, the Marquess of Norrington. I seem to recall your father writing me about your birth, but not much beyond that."

"I'm not sure what to say." Percival seemed truly flummoxed. "I was born. I grew up at our estate in Hertfordshire, and now I am reading classics at Oxford."

The earl grinned then laughed, the crinkles at the corners of his greenish-brown eyes adding a touch more to his handsome features. "That is a fine summary, my boy." He laid a hand on Percival's shoulder. "But what drives you? Why study the classics? What brings you to Nice, of all places?"

"Actually, my father thought I should visit. I wanted to go to Italy. He wanted me to go to Paris. So Nice was a compromise as he knew people—you, and a few others—here."

"Ah, Neville was not always one for compromise." Bemusement flashed in Berrick's eyes. "I see fatherhood has softened him somewhat."

"How do you know my father?"

"We were at school together, at Harrow. Then Oxford. Although, I admit, I was at Oxford for reasons other than studying. I think that was the beginning of the end of our close friendship."

"Did you have a falling out?"

"Not as such. More like our lives diverged. I enjoyed frivolity. Neville—Amesbury, rather, as he is a duke now—was so studious."

Bertram laughed. "Like father, like son."

Berrick beamed. "Good for you, my boy." He turned to Bertram. "And how do you know the marquess?"

"Bertie," Percival began, "or, rather, Bertram Atherley, the Viscount Ravensburgh—is a childhood friend. I used to play at his uncle's estate in St. Albans."

"However," said Bertram, "I'm a Cambridge man."

The earl guffawed. "Well, we all have our scandals. I fear my scandals drove me to France." He tossed his hands in the air. "And the glorious weather drove me to Nice."

"Yes," agreed Percival. "So very pleasant and perfect."

"You should really be here in winter when it truly is perfect. Which makes me wonder why you were here now. Usually we only see the tubercular or other invalids in these parts, and only in winter. You two strapping young men visiting in June is highly irregular."

Percival shifted on his feet revealing he was unprepared to answer such a question.

"My uncle in St. Albans died last month," Bertram offered. "The marquess and I felt a journey would help us in this period of grieving."

"Ah." Berrick nodded. "Invalids of the heart."

Bertram grunted. "Yes, I suppose."

"If you extend your stay during the summer, be forewarned. July and August are ever so sweltering. Which is why the invalids come here in the winter and return to England in the summer."

A handsome, dark-haired man, a bit older than Bertram, approached. He slipped his arm around the earl's waist.

Then he and the earl kissed each other. Just a peck on the lips, but lingering, and imbued with sentiment.

Bertram tensed. At his side, Percival stiffened.

The earl turned to them. "Gentlemen, may I introduce my François. He foolishly followed me from Paris a decade ago and has never left."

"Despite the sweltering summers," Bertram quipped.

François laughed heartily. He held out his hand. "I am François Bisset and pleased to make your acquaintance."

Introductions were made all around.

"And how do you two know each other?" François asked.

"We're the best of friends," offered Percival ingenuously.

The earl and François exchanged smiles as Bertram cringed a little. Was Percival that naïve?

"Are you here for the sea air?" asked François, his accented baritone seductively silky. "There is a wonderful beach cove where one can bathe and not be in the way of pesky fishermen."

"What if one wants to be in the way of a pesky fisherman?" the earl riposted.

As the two men laughed, Bertram found himself succumbing to their infectious mirth.

Despite a smile, Percival seemed a bit perplexed by the jocularity. "We would love to visit a beach. We've brought our bathing costumes."

"How grand," said Berrick. "I'll leave you in François's capable hands. He'll tell you about the cove, and introduce you all around." He patted François on the back then left to greet other guests.

"I would love to introduce you to Lady Suffield. But she has recently left the party for some unknown reason. Perhaps an assignation." François chuckled as if he had just told a joke. "She knows absolutely everyone in Nice."

"I thought Lord Berrick did, as well," Bertram replied.

"Basil only knows those who are worth knowing. Lady Suffield makes it her business to know even those who do not deserve our regard."

As they made their way across the room, François nodding and greeting guests along the way, Percival nudged Bertram.

"Bertie," he whispered, "the earl and François...are they...like us?"

"Later," Bertram said quietly. "We'll talk about it later."

~ INTERLUDE ~

The Adventures of Paolo the Pirate Hunter, the Magnificent Adventurer, who, along with his First Mate Barnaby, Protects the Seas from the Evil Pirate Jonas the Marauder

by Bertram Atherley, The Right Honorable 2nd Viscount Ravensburgh

Barnaby watched as the crew heaved up crates of fresh fruit from the pinnace bobbing in the water alongside the *Georgius*, dropping them to the deck. One crate hit the boards with such force the lid slid open, revealing the tufted, spiky fruit within. Barnaby had recently tasted such fruit, the sweet yet sour taste of the flesh a treat to his senses.

A sailor approached, a sharp knife in hand. "Would you like some, sir?"

The chap had read Barnaby's mind. "Yes, please."

Paolo sidled up on his left. "Are we ready to push on, Master Heath?" The captain always used the honorific when crew members were present.

"Yes, Captain. I do believe the last of the crates have been loaded. But first, you must take a moment to have a bite of this fruit."

"Oh?" Paolo studied the sailor as he sliced off the tuft of leaves from the top and began to peel the outer skin with his knife.

"Have you ever tasted it?" inquired Barnaby.

"No. Well, I don't think so."

"I'm certain you will enjoy it."

"What is it called?"

"I've heard it called many things," Barnaby explained. "Ananas or piña. But I do believe we English call it a pineapple."

"What an absolutely unusual name."

The sailor held out two slices of the yellow fruit. "The core is tough, like that of an apple, sir," he said to Paolo. "Just eat the ring of soft fruit around the core."

Barnaby took his slice and began to eat it, all the while watching Paolo first inspecting the slice, contemplating how he should confront it, then proceeding to eat it.

Paolo seemed surprised by the fruit's succulence and leaned forward to allow the juice to drip onto the deck as he ate. Barnaby restrained his amusement when his captain wiped his mouth on his sleeve, until Paolo looked up and met his gaze.

The two chuckled gleefully and hurled their remnant cores into the sea.

"Goodness, Master Heath, that was positively delectable."

Barnaby grinned. "And we have more in our stores, Captain. We are well stocked for our journey."

"And do we have our course, Master Heath?"

"Yes, Captain. We know where the *Jack Tar* is headed. We'll catch up to the blackguards when they least expect it."

Paolo wrapped his arm around Barnaby's shoulders. "Then let us forge ahead and stop this villainy."

~ * ~ * ~ * ~

CHAPTER TWELVE

Like Proteus, the mythological herdsman of the sea, a villain may assume any shape or form to elude capture, create havoc, or seduce the innocent.

— *The Adventures of Paolo the Pirate Hunter*

"You said we would talk about it."

Bertram sighed as he and Percival scrambled down the path to the secluded beach to which François had drawn a map with directions.

"When we're able to talk more privately," he said. "On the beach."

They had not yet had a chance to talk after the earl's extraordinary dinner the night before. They'd returned to the villa at two in the morning utterly exhausted, both needing time away from chatter and people, each desperate for sleep.

Morning had been too busy to have a meaningful conversation. The time until early afternoon was spent acquiring beach blankets and canvas folding chairs, gathering wide-brimmed hats and bathing costumes for their journey. Armand had sent them off with a knapsack stuffed with food and drink, which Percival wore, and helped fashion straps so Bertram could carry the chairs, blankets, and a sun umbrella on his back.

They took the horse tram as far as they could, then disembarked to walk the rest of the way, passing a few peasants, eventually meeting no one along the away.

A meadow frittered away into a rocky outcropping that led to a narrow path down to the shore.

"I think we're here." Bertram pulled the furniture off his sweaty back and plunked it down onto the white sand as he stared at the endless, shining sea.

"My God. That is the bluest water I have ever seen." Percival stood at his side.

"It is, isn't it?" Bertram drew in a breath, filling his nostrils with the salty, humid air. François had directed them to a paradise.

And they were utterly alone.

Bertram grasped Percival's hand and gave it a squeeze. Percival squeezed back, then quickly released his hold.

He set down his knapsack. "The water looks inviting. Especially since I'm perspiring like an Italian farm laborer."

Bertram guffawed as he shrugged out of his linen jacket. He unbuttoned his waistcoat, pulled off his braces, and stripped off his shirt. A gentle breeze cooled his heated skin, and sent a welcoming chill to ripple over him, momentarily giving him gooseflesh.

Percival stared, wide-eyed. Finally he blinked. "You didn't wear your bathing costume under your clothes?"

"What? No." Realization descended. "Oh. Did you?"

"I presumed there would be no bathing-huts."

Bertram unfurled a Turkish cotton beach blanket, releasing his bathing costume. "Will it bother you if I change in the open?" He glanced around. "We seem to be quite alone."

"Please. Go ahead."

Bertram plopped down on the blanket and took off his shoes and socks. When he stood to unbutton his trousers, Percival suddenly busied himself with setting up their chairs and umbrella, keeping his head down.

"It's all right if you look, Percy." Bertram pulled off his trousers. "I don't mind, you know."

With a sly smile, Percival watched as Bertram stepped into his bathing attire. "You're very brown for an Englishman," he said. "I mean on top. Especially your shoulders."

"When the weather is warm, sometimes I garden without a shirt." Bertram slid his arms into the sleeves, but left the placket unbuttoned.

"Without a shirt? Like a prehistoric man for all to see? What must the servants think?"

Bertram chuckled. "It's my property. And, unlike Wood Hall, we have very few servants. They seemingly do not care or are too spectacularly overworked to even notice. By the way, you are still in your clothes."

Percival removed his clothes, layer by layer. "I envy you your freedom. A duke's son could never run about half-dressed."

"You have such freedom now." Bertram enjoyed watching Percival undress, even if it wasn't all the way to the naked flesh. "And you can leave it unbuttoned." He pointed to Percival's costume. "Get some sun on you."

Percival unbuttoned the top few buttons. He beamed with a hint of satisfied accomplishment. "Shall we venture into the water?"

"Absolutely."

They strolled to the shore, stopping to let the gentle waves lap over their feet. The water was a little cool at first, but quickly became warm and inviting. Bertram forged ahead until he was waist deep.

Percival came up alongside. He glided his hands across the top of the water. "I've not been to the seashore since I was a child." He moved further until the water reached his chest and stared at the horizon.

Bertram followed, relishing the sensation of moving slowly while dancing on sand.

"The earl is like us, isn't he?" Percival asked quietly, as if someone could hear. "He prefers the company of men."

"Yes."

"And he knew my father."

"Yes."

"Which means my father has known of men such as us since before I was born."

There was pain in Percival's words, a pain Bertram wanted to soothe.

"I suppose so. But only if the earl had been forthcoming about his own preferences."

Percival turned to face him. "He said my father and he were close friends."

"And then they diverged."

"Perhaps that was why. Perhaps my father didn't approve of the earl. Didn't approve of such relationships."

"Or perhaps the earl tried to seduce your father?"

Percival grimaced. "That's a disconcerting thought. One does not want to know about one's parents in that way."

"Oh, I don't know about that. I love hearing stories about my mother and father. She was so happy with him, as I recall. But she didn't have much time with him."

"Such a tragedy." Percival looked down at Bertram's chest. He drew a finger along the vee of the open placket. He licked his lips, as his breaths quickened in an unsteady rhythm.

Was the marquess leaning forward? It seemed so, but the bright sunlight and the gently lapping waves were distorting his senses. Bertram restrained himself, holding as still as could be.

Percival lifted his gaze to Bertram's mouth. Little puffs of breath fanned over Bertram's chin.

He really was drawing closer. An invitation. Surely it was. It had to be. A shivering thrill livened his cock.

Bertram angled forward. "Percy, we shouldn't stand too closely. I mean, only because if people know we know the earl—"

Percival stepped back. "Sorry. I wasn't thinking. It's just so perfectly lovely here. With you."

He arched over to lay on his back and, with arms flailing in the water, slowly swam toward the horizon, his expression soft and serene.

As if he felt safe. Percival deserved to feel safe. That he felt safe with Bertram was heartening.

Bertram swam out to meet him.

"Oh, Bertie, isn't wonderful? To move one's limbs in utter abandon. To let the water cradle one's body in its embrace." Percival breathed in. "I feel so alive."

"Is it better than Italy?"

Percival gaped, then guffawed. "Not better. Different. Italy was inspiring to my mind, my intellect. The endless sea just makes one feel there are endless possibilities for life itself."

He bobbed, then disappeared under the water.

A tug on the hem of Bertram's bathing suit sent him under the surface.

Percival smiled through puffed cheeks, his blond hair suspended in the water with wild abandon, like some impish sea-creature. He grabbed Bertram's shoulders and drew him close.

Then kissed him on his puckered mouth.

Surprise was fleeting as Percival swam away. Bertram followed, catching up once his feet hit the sand, the water at his shoulders.

Perfect for standing. Together. "I have an idea."

Percival turned slowly in the water. "Oh?" He tugged on his lower lip with his teeth.

"Wrap your legs around my waist."

His eyes widened, furrowing his brow.

"We'll be connected, but we can lean away."

"All right. Catch."

Percival jumped up, opening his legs, swirling water in their wake. Bertram grabbed his calves, then, little by little, danced his fingers along the underside of Percival's knees, his thighs, until he reached the hem of his bathing suit. Percival sighed as he wrapped his legs around Bertram's waist and leaned back onto the water.

Pleasure wrested a gasp from Bertram's lungs as his erection nestled ever so comfortably in the cleft of Percival's butt.

A raised eyebrow and a grin were Percival's accession that he knew Bertram's motivations. But pleasure should be for both, not just for one.

"May I touch you?"

A blush not from the heat of the afternoon sun dusted Percival's cheeks. "Yes. Please."

Bertram grasped Percival's hips, steadying him as he rocked his own, then palmed the marquess's cock, rubbing the hard length through the wet fabric.

Arms wide and gently paddling, Percival floated on the water, his expression of contentment the only encouragement Bertram needed.

He rubbed his erection along Percival's delicious cleft, twinges of tightening muscles spurring him on. God, how he wanted to just thrust his hips like they were actually fucking until both came.

But that would agitate the water too much. It would draw too much attention.

A chill of panic swept over him. As much as he wanted— needed—the intimacy, here was not the place. They were too exposed, too public. Even at a secluded beach.

He stopped all movement.

"Percy, we shouldn't. Not here."

Percival raised his head and met his gaze, his eyes glazed. He blinked, then pushed away, laughing as waves of water curled over his outstretched arms. He quickly paddled back. "And now I have an idea, my dear viscount."

He returned to shore, grabbed his straw hat, then proceeded to fuss with the blanket and the umbrella, seemingly trying to maximize the arc of shade. He stood back and reviewed his efforts, nodded, then beckoned to Bertram, and lay down on the blanket.

Bertram took his place at his side, propping himself up on his elbows. They were shielded from the cliffs, alone in a private cocoon.

"How very clever."

Percival drew circles with his finger over the back of Bertram's hand, then turned it over to continue the sensual touch on his palm.

"Your hands are more calloused than mine." Was there a quiver in Percival's voice?

"All that gardening."

"Yes." As Percival's hand curled around Bertram's palm, he leaned forward, lips parting, and flicked the tip of his tongue tentatively along the seam of Bertram's mouth.

In a dizzying whirl, the beach, the sun, the water, the world slipped away.

Bertram closed his eyes and exhaled as he dared deepen the kiss. He had dreamed of this moment since the night in the carriage, yet had purposefully restrained his enthusiasm. Percival was still fragile, his emotions still delicate.

And yet, Percival was willingly kissing him, his free hand now tangling fingertips in the hair of Bertram's chest.

My God, it was happening. After all these weeks, all these *years*, finally happening. Percy, *his* Percy, was finally really his.

Heaven, this was pure heaven. He could stay in this moment for eternity, kissing, touching, the melody of waves and sea birds the accompaniment to their romantic interlude.

Abruptly, Percival drew back, patting Bertram's chest. "Thank you, Bertie, for being such a patient friend."

What should one say in response? "Of course."

"Now, I do believe there is a fine luncheon and an even better bottle of wine to be had."

Joy provoked Bertram's laugh. Definitely France was turning out to be better than Italy.

Percival sighed as he strolled into the sitting room between their bedrooms. He stood at the balcony doors gazing at the view of the Mediterranean.

The day at the beach had been magical. He'd spent the afternoon with his best friend, pushing the boundaries of their friendship.

"I am quite frazzled." Bertram joined him at the French doors with a sigh. He tore off his jacket as if to punctuate his point.

They locked gazes. Bertram's brown eyes sparkled in a countenance that suggested contentment. A reflection of what he himself felt.

"I know I just took a nap on the beach, but I'm ready for another before dinner."

Bertram chuckled. "I think I will avail myself of the inconsistent indoor plumbing and take a bath." He smiled then exited through the door to his bedroom.

Percival leaned against the door jamb.

Being in Bertram's arms that afternoon had been a fantasy come to life. His embrace had been thrilling and comforting, his kiss enlivening and subduing. Percival had forgotten the world around them, then, upon closing his eyes, let all sensation focus on the joining of their mouths.

Until a flicker of a nightmare had flashed in his mind's eye, convincing him he was in Jack's arms fantasizing about Bertram.

He couldn't continue after that. The fear of dredging up more memories persisted. So he'd suggested luncheon.

Bertram had been an important part of why the afternoon had been so special. He had been cordial, gentlemanly, funny, and, yes, erotic, all of which had left Percival with a sort of indistinct, warm, drowsy happiness.

Jack had never elicited such feelings.

Jack had never been special.

No, he'd been positively monstrous.

When Percival had been with Jack, he'd always felt the exact opposite. Anxious, apprehensive, filled with not just a little dread. And never truly happy, even though he thought he might be, could be, eventually. Especially when Jack had not been drinking.

But Jack was always drinking.

Percival straightened with a shudder and went to the door to his bedroom, the sudden chill chafing his flesh making a hot bath sound like a very good idea, indeed.

A hand fell on his shoulder, pulling, propelling him backward. He struggled, shoving his assailant with a yelp and the strength only fear could muster. The blackguard fell onto the rug with a thud.

"Percy?"

Bollocks. Bertie. Oh God, what had he done? Percival gaped at his friend, panic gripping his heart.

Bertram was sprawled inelegantly on the carpet, legs bent and open, his nudity exposed by the split of his dressing gown now askew.

"Bertie, my God, Bertie. I apologize. I..." He screwed his eyes shut squeezing out the pain before recovering. "Jesus. I thought you Jack."

A touch of incredulity darkened Bertram's expression for a fleeting moment. "I understand, Percy," he said, overly calm. "I should not have presumed. I should have asked before I...attempted anything."

Percival offered a hand to help Bertram up.

The sitting room door crashed open.

"Monsieur!"

Damn and blast. Not Blandine. What the hell was she doing here?

She ran to him, then grasped him in an awkward embrace.

"*Avez-vous été blessé?*" She stared daggers at a now standing Bertram.

Percival shrugged her off. "No. No. I am unharmed." He pointed to the door. "*Quitte cette pièce. Tout de suite.*"

She looked as if she were about to cry at his harsh instruction for her to leave.

"*Si te plait,*" he added reluctantly. Saying *please* should soften the blow.

She skulked out, closing the door behind her, but not without a cross glance Bertram's way.

Percival locked the sitting room door as Bertram straightened and re-tied his dressing gown.

"She's got quite the case on you, you know."

"I do know and it is terribly unsettling." Almost as unsettling as his thoughts of Jack had been.

Bertram offered a sympathetic smile. "Well, I thought, perhaps, we could take that nap together."

There was that cozy feeling again. "Or a bath?"

That set them both to laughing.

"But probably not such a good idea." Bertram shifted on his slippered feet.

"I suppose not. Especially with the maid lurking about."

"Yeah." Bertram smiled. "So I'll see you at dinner, then?"

"Absolutely."

Percival watched as Bertram returned to his room, a faint impression of the curve of the viscount's buttocks under the silk of his dressing gown enlivening his fantasies.

Dinner with Bertram had been simple and delightful. But of course it had been. Being with Bertram was so easy and always entertaining.

Percival sat in the window seat of his bedroom and gazed out at the shaft of moonlight shimmering on the Mediterranean Sea. The same sea they had frolicked in earlier that day, the memory of which still burned in his brain like the sun beating down upon the water.

And left him pondering more fantasies of him and Bertram together.

He had never actually fantasized about Bertram while he'd been with Jack. He hadn't really thought of Bertram in a libidinous way at that time. The viscount was simply his childhood friend Bertie. But even if he had been attracted to Bertram, he could have never got away with such thoughts. Jack controlled every part of his life, his actions in real life, and his thoughts and fantasies in his own mind.

But he was free, now, wasn't he? Free to fantasize about his best friend, fantasize even without his best friend knowing the lustful extent of his desires.

Percival pulled up the hem of his nightshirt and wrapped his hand around his already stiffening cock.

What Bertram had done that afternoon had been positively exhilarating. The double pleasure of the viscount's hand cupping his erection, while his own hard prick had massaged along Percival's cleft had been dizzying. Adding to that the warmth of the sun and the rhythm of the waves, and, for one minute, he had experienced all that heaven itself must have to offer.

Percival closed his eyes, the half-moon still casting its moody light through his lids, and concentrated on his hand pumping along his shaft. Such a wonderful experience to give oneself pleasure while thinking of another who added to that pleasure.

If only the umbrella could have been in the water, shielding them from any onlookers, they could have continued with their folly. Bertram would have continued to grip Percival's cock while focusing on his own pleasure, rubbing his cock against Percival, while the waves would have lapped around them in a sensual embrace.

Eventually, as he approached his own culmination, Bertram would have had to release his hold. No bother. Percival would have simply gripped his own shaft, knowing precisely how to bring himself off.

Slowly…slowly…picking up the pace a little more quickly, then just letting go, coming in the water at the same time Bertram let loose underneath him.

Percival opened his eyes, his smile unstoppable.

He wiped his emission from his hand and prick with his nightshirt then leaned against the wall of the alcove and exhaled.

Drowsiness tugged at his eyelids. He almost did not want to bother climbing into bed, but he'd have a terrific crick in his neck if he slept that way all night.

He got up and slid into bed, knowing slumber would soon take him on a journey to sensual dreams in his relaxed state.

A MUFFLED CLANG juddered Bertram awake, disorientation stilling him for a moment. He lay on his back, his hand on his cock.

Right. Retiring to his bed after dinner, he had drifted off to sleep while wondering whether or not he was too tired to masturbate.

The noise was probably Percival remembering to lock the door to their suite.

He turned onto his side, the need for sleep overpowering his need for release now that the disturbance had subdued his motivation.

He closed his eyes.

A shriek shattered the stillness.

His lids flew open, but his body remained frozen. Had it been a woman's scream? Outside?

He listened. The silence of the night was deafening.

Until it wasn't.

"Get out!"

Percy. That was Percival's voice.

He leaped out of bed, grabbed his dressing gown to cover his nakedness, and bolted for Percival's bedroom, wrenching the door open.

The dim glow of a bedside lamp revealed Percival, wearing only his nightshirt and a terrified expression, plastered up against the far wall.

Blandine stood on the other side of the bed, crying, clutching clothes to her semi-nude body.

Why the hell was she undressed?

Oh, good God.

Percival pointed at her. "Get that woman out of here."

Armand burst through the door, taking in the scene. Bertram nodded in the direction of Blandine, as he himself went to Percival, shielding him. Percival's frantic breaths filled his ear.

Very slowly, Armand approached the maid. *"Viens avec moi, Blandine,"* he said, beckoning her to go to him. *"Laisse le marquis. Il y a une autre, une autre femme dans son coeur."*

Leave the marquess alone. There is another woman in his heart.

Somehow that convinced her. She left with Armand, her head hung down.

Bertram did not move until he heard the snick of the suite door and the key turn in the lock.

Percival slumped against the wall and sagged to the floor. Bertram knelt at his side.

"Percy, are you all right?"

"Yes. I think so." He drew in a long inhalation, then exhaled, then did it all over again more slowly. He placed his hand on his heart. "I just need to calm myself." He looked up at Bertram. "She was in my bed, Bertie. Naked. She touched me. It was horrifying."

"Can you stand?"

"Yes."

Bertram helped him up. "How about, just for tonight—" he couldn't believe he was about to say what he was going to say "—you sleep in my bed?"

Percival passed a shaking hand over his brow. "All right," he said with a touch of enervation.

Bertram doused the lamp, then guided Percival to his own room. While Percival got into the bed, he positioned an easy chair near the window, facing the closed door.

"Will you stay with me?"

"Yes, I'll be right here." Bertram tightened the sash around his waist.

"No, I mean, in bed with me?"

A frisson of surprise crept across Bertram's skin. "Are you certain?"

"I need someone to keep me safe. I need to feel safe." Percival sighed. "God, I was not expecting that…expecting her. It just brought back memories of…"

"I understand," Bertram said quickly as he climbed onto to mattress. The bed shook as he settled himself on his side.

Percival slid toward him. "Hold me."

Bertram wrapped an arm around him, being careful to keep space between their hips.

It was no use, though. Percival nestled his entire body against him. Moments later his breathing held the rhythm of sleep.

While Bertram's crotch thrummed erratically in desperate need.

CHAPTER THIRTEEN

*A sailor in distress may find himself in the embrace of a Nereid, a
sea-nymph, his protector who will buoy him as he navigates an
open expanse of sea.*
— *The Adventures of Paolo the Pirate Hunter*

Percival did not know what to expect when he and Bertram
went down for breakfast the morning after...*the incident.*

Armand had not appeared as expected, so Percival had to
dress by himself, all the while Bertram, far more adept at self-
grooming, watched as he waited for him.

"Are you certain you don't need my help, my lord?"

Percival had ignored the teasing in his voice. "I can manage,
my dear viscount."

But their walk down the stairs to the breakfast room was in
silence. They glanced at each other as they strolled through the
double doors.

A young man whom they had never seen before busied about adjusting silverware and serviettes. He looked up as they entered, the soft angles of his face betraying his youthfulness.

He beamed, then bowed. "Good morning, my lords," he said in a melodic tenor, his English holding only the merest French lilt. Smooth cheeks anchored a mouth of plump lips. His physique was unusual for a man. Slim but with a cinched waist more conventional for a woman.

"Good morning," said Bertram as he went to the buffet and grabbed a plate, clearly unfazed by the presence of an unfamiliar servant in their midst.

"And you are?" Percival asked.

"I am Claude. Monsieur Armand requested my presence this morning. It was very short notice, so I apologize if the breakfast is not as expected."

"It looks wonderful, Claude," said Bertram, still clearly unvexed by the remarkable situation. "The coffee smells divine."

Armand entered. "Ah, my lords Norrington and Ravensburgh, I see you have met our new butler." He smiled cordially. "Claude, this is the Marquess of Norrington and the Viscount Ravensburgh."

Bertram nodded as he chewed whatever he was grazing on from his adventures at the buffet.

Percival raised a brow in Armand's direction. "And how do you know Claude?"

"I apologize, my lord. I dismissed the Frossards last night. I made some inquiries with Lord Berrick and Monsieur Bisset early this morning about hiring more appropriate servants." He lingered on the word *appropriate*, as if that held a particular meaning.

Percival regarded Claude one more time. The smiling youth had a fresh beauty that seemed very…feminine.

Oh. Of course. He'd heard that some men of their ilk were effeminate. "Yes, I see. Thank you, Armand."

"I thought breakfast the most pressing issue of the day. I will see to other servants presently." Armand bowed and left.

"Do you have everything you require?" asked the deferential Claude.

"Yes," said Bertram as he put down his rather full plate. He pulled out a chair and sat.

"Yes," Percival agreed.

Claude smiled again and left, his hips twitching just a tad under his nipped-in waist.

Percival surveyed the buffet and its marvelous array of breakfasting opportunities. He'd start slow, with some coffee, eggs, perhaps a pastry.

"Bertie," he said quietly as he took his seat, "I'm not certain if Claude is a man or a woman."

Bertram wiped his mouth with a linen serviette and shrugged. "Does it matter?"

Oh. "I…I suppose not. I just have never encountered such a person."

"There are more things in heaven and earth than are dreamt of in your philosophy." Bertram winked.

"That's Shakespeare, isn't it?"

A smile presaged a forkful of breakfast. "Very astute for one who studies Etruscans."

Percival sat and attended his own plate.

There were indeed many possibilities of how one could live beyond convention. Had they just been given an opportunity to explore those possibilities?

If so, how on earth should one proceed?

Not long after breakfast, Armand had ushered Bertram and Percival out of the villa, packing them off to town, to the beach. "Anywhere. *Je me fiche de savoir où*—I don't care where," he'd said. Armand needed time to find new staff.

"I think he's rather excited for this opportunity," Percival had observed.

"He did not get on well with Madame Frossard," Bertram had agreed. "Really, they did not even try to hide their animosity toward each other."

Unwelcome at the villa, and not wanting to tempt fate with any unexpected encounters with the Frossards, the two had escaped via tram then on foot to what they considered their own private resort.

Inwardly, Bertram was filled with excited glee. Percival at the beach was a bit more free than Percival in the villa. Perhaps with replacement servants—especially if Claude was any indication—Percival would eventually feel more free at the villa, as well. Bertram would have to just wait and see.

His prick, of course, was thoroughly impatient.

They hiked down the hill to the beach, arriving at the moment two rather attractive—and shirtless—Frenchmen were packing up fishing gear and pulling up their boat.

"Oh, my," Percival said under his breath. "The canonical fishermen."

Indeed. Muscles flexing as they worked shirtless. Skin bronzed by hours and days under the sun. One man had sun-kissed blond streaks in his curls. Both laughed at some private diversion.

"They look as if fishing were not their trade but rather an avocation." Percival's voice held astonishment.

"Perhaps it's not. Perhaps they are two friends who were out on a boat."

"With quite a bit of fishing equipment."

"Yes, true." Bertram had to agree. Were their trousers a bit tight around their perfect butts, or was that just his imagination? "It is late in the morning. I imagine fishermen would be fishing quite a bit earlier?"

"I have absolutely no idea," Percival said slowly as he continued to stare.

They should not be staring. "Percy, we should not be staring."

Percival's lips widened into a discerning smile. "But we are merely tourists. We are observing scenes we do not have at home."

Bertram chuckled and continued to the spot they had occupied the day before. He nodded a greeting to the fishermen as the bronzed paragons looked in their direction. The fishermen nodded back with broad grins.

Probably amused the aristocrats were carrying the accoutrements of leisure and not the equipment of labor.

Such judgments did not affect Bertram, especially not at that moment. He inhaled the salty air, delighting in the warmth of the sun on his pallid English cheeks, and watched as the fishermen began the climb back to civilization.

Percival dropped the picnic hamper on the sand. "Do you think pirate hunters had time to enjoy the sun and blue waters of the Caribbean?"

Bertram chuckled. "I imagine anyone from dreary England would find the blue seas and white sands of the Caribbean a glorious fantastical place."

"Have you ever been?"

"I admit I have not."

"But you write as if you know what it must be like."

Pride curled Bertram's lips. "I have only succeeded in convincing you I know what it must be like."

Percival laughed then proceeded to unpack their beach gear, setting up the umbrella and spreading out the blankets. "If you ask me, I think you should allow Paolo and Barnaby the time to enjoy the delights of the tropics." He began to undress. "All of the ship's crew, really."

That Percival was involved with the story was heartwarming. "Would they be wearing bathing costumes?" Bertram asked as he shuffled out of his clothes.

"I should think not," Percival said stripping off his waistcoat. "Paolo is an adventurer. He does not have time for such frippery as bathing attire."

Whereas two Englishmen in Nice apparently did require such specialized attire. Well, only because one of said Englishmen had good reason to be circumspect. There was freedom in nudity, but

Percival was possibly not quite ready to reveal himself. So Bertram followed along. Once down to his drawers, he turned his back to Percival and grabbed his beach robe, wrapping the cotton fabric around him before he stripped off his undergarments. He grabbed his knapsack and searched for his swimming costume.

"Percy, did I pack my bathing costume in my bag or yours?" Bertram looked up, expecting an answer, and instead saw a most exquisite sight.

Before him Percival stretched, unabashedly revealing his sleek and supple nude body to the sun, sea, sky—and Bertram.

"You're not wearing your bathing costume," Bertram blurted. "I mean, under your clothes."

"I didn't really have time, did I? Not with Armand marshaling us out so quickly. At least Claude packed us off with victuals and wine." Percival reached his arms overhead, his stones gently swaying between splayed legs, then bent down and extended himself on a portion of blanket in the full sun.

Bertram positioned his body to shield the marquess's face from the rays. "Be careful or you'll turn as brown as a fisherman. We have dinner at Lady Suffield's tonight."

An irked groan was the answer.

"At least cover your face with your hat so your nose doesn't burn."

Percival grabbed his straw hat and placed it over his face. A moment later, he lifted it. "Join me in getting brown."

"I think not." *Your nude body is too enticing.* "I need to cool off after our walk."

"Then shall we enjoy the water a spell before napping under the sun?"

Still leery of Percival's new-found confidence, Bertram countered, "We should dress for the occasion, no?"

A mischievous gleam shone in Percival's eyes. "Let us greet Poseidon as Greek warriors."

Good God. Was Percival intending to swim naked?

They *were* quite alone. And the beach was relatively secluded. "All right."

Percival jumped up and ran to the shore, dancing a bit at the water's edge before plowing onward, diving into a wave. He re-emerged with a yowl and a shake of his head, his wet hair whipping out a spiral of droplets.

With a laugh, Bertram tore off his drawers and his robe and ran to the shore, diving and swimming as quickly as possible to water high enough to hide his burgeoning arousal. Churning his legs, he bobbed at Percival's side, the sun on his back, the warm water, and the nearness of the marquess teasing his senses.

"This is precisely what I meant about your pirate hunters." Percival paddled in place. "Swimming free in the water, not caring about the world. Just a couple of mates relaxing." With closed eyes, he lifted his face to the sun, then laid back onto the water, floating on the top for a brief spell, his half-hard cock above the surface. He drifted in front of Bertram. He turned his face, their lips almost touching.

"Thank you for harboring me in your bed last night."

"Percy, you don't have to thank me. I'm here for you whenever you need me."

With a little splash, Percival scrambled to a vertical position. "I'm still fragile, Bertie. But I find being with you so incredibly intoxicating." He leaned forward and gave him a peck on the lips.

Bertram wrapped an arm around Percival's slim waist, steering them both to where they could stand, then gently urging their hips together.

Percival nipped on his lower lip. Under the water his erection nudged Bertram's.

"You know all too well how to drive me mad with lust."

"I do." Percival blushed.

This was neither the time nor place for such provocative playfulness. "Perhaps we can continue this game later?"

"Of course." Percival shook his head as if waking from a dream. A crease trembled and deepened between his brows. "I think I just want to swim now. With you. I want to be with you. I want us to be together. I need you to be at my side. As my friend."

"You know I am your friend, Percy. I have always been your friend. Ever since that day Nicky and I found you wandering around the Atherley estate."

Percival beamed—whether at the memory, or at Bertram's assurance, was not clear. His smile tore at Bertram's heart. Under all the pain there was still a shred of joy.

"Yes," Bertram agreed. "Let us swim as friends."

For now.

CHAPTER FOURTEEN

How strange it was to meet citizens of Britannia living on the shores of another island as if they were exiles and not settlers.
— *The Adventures of Paolo the Pirate Hunter*

Percival stared out the window of the hired carriage, the drama of the sunset softened by wispy streaks of pale gray against the vibrant orange and pink sky. The scene for that evening's entertainment was the extravagant mansion of the Countess of Suffield, another English expatriate, and somehow a friend of Father's.

"Maybe they had an affair," Bertram surmised.

"I doubt that. She's in her seventies, I believe. That makes her at least twenty or more years older than Father." He pondered such a liaison. "I suppose he had a life before he married Mother."

"Older women have desires of the flesh, I imagine. And younger men are often quite willing." Bertram turned a sly smile his direction.

Percival cringed. "I do not want to know about such things. Especially as concerns my father."

Bertram laughed. Percival leaned against him. Bertram wrapped an arm around his shoulder.

They stayed that way—comfortable, silent, gratified—until they arrived at Lady Suffield's house. The pale stone façade glowed with the golds of dusk, the Neoclassical portico giving the provincial edifice a sophisticated elegance. In the middle of the circular drive stood a tiered fountain with putti lounging on the rims of the wide bowls, and crowned by a spouting dolphin. Percival and Bertram alighted quickly as a line of carriages waited behind them. Footmen stood guard as they stepped over the threshold of the front door and entered, the act casual, with no receiving line or announcement of their presence.

The foyer opened onto a grand marble-clad gallery. Percival contained a gasp as he surveyed the glorious space.

Apparently Lady Suffield had a fondness for the ancients. Everywhere was some decorative element pertaining to the Greeks or Romans. Sculptures of marble or bronze, mosaic floors, and painted walls were a feast to the eye. Were they authentic? It did not matter. The effect was paradisiacal for one who studied ancient art and style.

"I imagine you and the countess will get on famously," Bertram said with a chuckle.

"I do believe I agree with that assessment."

"Lord Norrington!"

The two turned at the enthusiastic call from an approaching woman. Gray-haired and slender, she wore a crimson gown draped generously across her person. She stopped before them, her pale brown eyes studying Percival for a moment before she took his hands.

"You are indeed Neville's son. I see the resemblance."

Percival smiled politely.

"Oh, but I forget myself in my excitement." She let go of Percival. "Thank you for accepting my invitation, Lord

Norrington. I am Cora Wilby, the Countess of Suffield, at your service."

She seemed so much younger than a woman in her seventies. "Pleased to make your acquaintance, Lady Suffield." He nodded deferentially.

"How so very like Neville you are." She assessed him up and down with a smile, then shook her head as if awakening. "I beg your pardon. You must be wondering how I know your family."

"I will admit I am, my lady."

"In my younger days—" she laughed softly, "well, younger than I am now—I was what one might call a 'matchmaker'. It was all rather informal, although for very formal reasons. Some families needed an intermediary when it came to marrying off their progeny. Your grandfather requested my assistance. I facilitated the introduction between your father and your mother."

Percival tried to contain his shock. Apparently not very well.

"You needn't look so surprised, my lord. I know the fashion today tends towards romantical notions of two young people in love. But a generation ago, we English were still rather medieval. And some men of the *ton* needed more help than others."

"Then I must thank you for my very existence, my lady."

She laughed, jiggling the fantastical ornament shaped like a Greco-Roman temple that clung to the side of her swept-up hair. Only then did she glance at Bertram, who had all along held a polite smile. "Oh. You've brought a friend. And you are?"

"Bertram Atherley, the Viscount Ravensburgh, my lady," he said with a slight bow. "At your service."

"Atherley? Any relation to the St. Albans Atherleys?"

"The late Earl of St. Albans was my uncle. My father's brother."

"Ah, I only knew *of* him. I never met the man. But now you say he is dead?"

"In May, my lady," he said. "So I took the opportunity to travel with the marquess. I find the distance and the sunshine helps while mourning."

She cast a polite smile in Bertram's direction. "We exiles all find the sunshine restorative to our hearts and minds."

Exiles?

Lady Suffield turned to Percival. "Lord Norrington, you must meet my granddaughters Leah and Annette. They are visiting from England." She sighed. "I suspect they are a little bored with my friends and would love to talk to someone more their own age."

"Of course, my lady. I would be delighted," Percival said pleasantly despite niggling suspicions. The lady *had* once been a matchmaker.

"But first, my lords, please have some refreshment." She gestured grandly. "There are servants about with trays of wonderful French wines. And please feel free to venture into the dining room. We are offering supper on the buffet, my version of a rather casual *service à la française*. You don't even have to sit at the dining table."

After a graceful bow of her head so as not to upset her ornament, she departed, waving and calling out to her next guest.

"My dear Percival, you do look as if you have seen a ghost."

"She said exile."

Bertram knitted his brow, nonplussed. "She did, I suppose."

Percival scowled at Bertram. "She said exile," he hissed under his breath. "Not expatriate."

"I'm not sure I follow."

"Bertie, these English friends of my father's—Lord Berrick and Lady Suffield—are not in the south of France for their health. For some reason they felt they needed to leave England for a more favorable location."

Bertram blinked. "Let's fetch some glasses of that fine French wine and discuss this in a private corner somewhere."

Wine procured, they ensconced themselves outside at the wall on the edge of the garden. A view of the Mediterranean glittering in the early twilight was their backdrop, exotic flowers and palms set the scene.

Percival was compelled to take a generous draught of wine.

"Percy, do you think your father was perhaps more than just friends with Berrick?"

Damnation. "Yes, and someone knew of the liaison, hence Lady Suffield was brought in to find a more suitable mate."

"A woman."

"My mother." Percival exhaled, then gulped more wine, the dry fruitiness numbing his senses. "To cover up his secret life."

Bertram stared at him, a touch of concern wrinkling between his eyebrows. "I want to remind you that you are merely speculating all of this."

He was. "I am."

"Perhaps your father found Lady Suffield utterly charming when she was finding a wife for him and became friendly. Or," he held the word with dramatic effect, "perhaps she made a horrible match for another denizen of the aristocracy and was drummed out of England by the *ton*. Perhaps your father told her of an old boyhood chum—Berrick—who lived in Nice and that she should visit and make her acquaintance to him. Perhaps none of what you fear is true. Perhaps there is another explanation."

He was right, by God. Bertram was right. He had a talent to perceive all possibilities. Because he was a writer and could see all aspects of a story.

"Thank you." Percival finished his wine. "I needed to hear some other drama than that which was playing out in my damned brain."

"I'm glad I could offer some assistance. Now, Percy, I'm famished, and I suspect you are as well. Let's get something from the buffet. And then you must be your charming self and converse with Lady Suffield's granddaughters."

Bertram was right. He *was* famished. Food might help calm his body, his brain, and his aching soul.

LADY SUFFIELD'S supper had been casual only in the manner most were partaking of it, not in the epicurean variety of the dishes. The savory pies and sandwiches were small enough to eat with one or two bites, the fruit salads and vegetables could be eaten with only a fork—no knife needed. As such, many guests remained standing as they ate.

Bertram had been famished and decided to eat perpendicular so he could easily return to the buffet. With a plate piled quite high, Percival had decided to sit, joining a small group of matrons at a table.

After Claude's breakfast, they hadn't had much of a luncheon—really just the remains of breakfast hastily packed into the hamper. And there had been no afternoon tea. Armand had needed all day to assemble the new household staff.

Now satiated, Bertram sipped a smoky whiskey in the drawing room. Percival had finally met Lady Suffield's granddaughters and sat between the two adolescents on a snug antique sofa. He laughed genuinely at some story they were telling him. He looked as if he were actually enjoying himself.

"Our little community in Nice is rather welcoming, *n'est-ce pas?*" Berrick pulled up a chair next to Bertram and sat, holding a glass of amber liquor.

"You have carved out an agreeable niche. A home away from home." Bertram eyed him. "Have you been back?"

"To England?" The earl reacted in surprise. "I have. Many times. Only briefly, though. I am still officially a member of the House of Lords." He emitted a snort. "However, my home is here now." He sipped his liquor. "François is here."

Exiles, not expatriates.

Berrick's mien softened. "I hear from my *majordome* that he helped your man Monsieur Armand Thibaut acquire more—" he leaned in a little "—appropriate servants during your stay."

Bertram raised his glass. "Please convey our gratitude to your butler. We had some difficulties with the previous staff."

"Yes, despite French law being more tolerant of our kind, traditions and intolerance do still persist." He swirled then sipped his liquor.

Did Berrick suspect he and Percival were more than friends? Bertram stared at his whiskey. They were more than just friends, weren't they? If his unsatisfied cock had anything to say about it, only sort of.

"I'm glad Lord Norrington has deigned to entertain Lady Leah and Lady Annette. They often find themselves at Cora's soirées with no children their own age. Well, I suppose they're not really children anymore. How old is Lord Norrington?"

"Twenty-one."

"Ah. Leah is seventeen and Annette is sixteen. He's the closest in age to them at this whole affair." The earl chuckled softly as he watched the trio. "They're like children at play."

Indeed, they were, albeit on a gilded neoclassical sofa. Percival was animated, laughing, making faces, the two girls responding with their own. As if he were a child again among playmates.

Bertram's heart warmed yet worried at the sight. Was Percival gaining enough confidence to break free of his past? Or was he trying to return to a previous time before any trauma had happened?

"I admit such displays are why I love our group of societal *refusées*," continued Berrick. "It's so refreshing to see young women act their age instead of following some expected convention of what is considered lady-like behavior. That will be their fate soon enough back home in England." He sighed and finished the contents of his glass.

Percival's fate as well.

The earl stood. "If Cora hasn't yet invited you, please do explore her house and the garden. The garden especially is quite exquisite."

"I have seen some of it, and I agree." Bertram smiled. "The exotic plants may be what bring me back again and again."

The earl grinned, winked, and took his leave.

Bertram finished his whiskey, then glanced in Percival's direction. The marquess was still having the time of his life. The scene was encouraging. Perhaps Percival was indeed beginning to move beyond his past sufferings.

After a servant relieved him of his glass, Bertram stood and ventured outside to the garden.

The day's humidity lingered in the cool night air, the deep blue of night clung to the sky. A few lights in the distance were reminders of the presence of the small town huddled against the shore. Behind him, gaslight chandeliers and the hum of discourse reminded him of social pleasantries. He inhaled deeply, the tang of salt in the air reminding him of his current wonderful existence.

"Bon soir, monsieur."

Bertram turned at the sound of the woman's voice. *"Bon soir,"* he greeted his good evening in return.

"C'est une belle vue, n'est-ce pas?"

A beautiful view. *"Oui.* Although the view was more spectacular during sunset."

"Ah, you are English." She approached more closely. She smiled, the light from the house revealing the subtle lines of an older woman. Perhaps in her forties.

"I am."

She studied him. "You are new to Nice, *n'est-ce pas?"*

"Yes. I and my countryman are recently arrived." No need to be utterly truthful to a stranger at a party.

"Ah, then you know the young Englishman chatting with Lady Suffield's granddaughters?" She wrapped her arm around his and led him toward a group of shrubs trimmed in geometric shapes.

"I do. He is a close friend and my traveling companion."

"He is very polite. And quite handsome."

Bertram chuckled. "I suppose he is. Especially when he is in the company of such lovely girls."

She smoothed some unseen crease on her skirt. "How do you know him?"

"He used to play on my uncle's property."

A light breeze wafted her perfume in the air. Roses with a hint of orange blossom. "Oh? Was he so poor that he had to visit you and your uncle to play?"

"Rather the opposite. His father's estate was well-maintained and well-manicured, like Lady Suffield's. My uncle's land was rather natural and unkempt. Perhaps 'romantic' is a more diplomatic word."

The woman laughed softly. "And why are you here in Nice? You do not seem as invalids."

"My friend's father knows Lady Suffield. He thought we should call upon her while we are on the continent."

With a swish of her skirts, she pulled him into the shadow between two topiaries. "And is this handsome young man married?"

"Not yet. Perhaps you know of a lonely princess?"

She laughed softly. "*Non*, I do not. I am a mere, how do you say? *Veuve*."

"Widow." He offered a slight bow of his head. "My sympathies."

"Oh, *non*, it has been a very long time. And he was not so much a gentleman." She smiled with lips parted, then dragged the tip of her tongue across the edges of her upper teeth.

Good God. Was she trying to seduce him?

"And you?" She placed her hand over his heart. "Are you married?"

Indeed, she was trying to seduce him.

"No."

"I am surprised. Has no one struck your fancy?" Her fingers danced down the lapel of his jacket, then lingered at a button.

Bertram froze. He'd never been seduced by a woman. "Something like that. I suppose I keep to myself too much. I'm rather bookish."

"Oh, but a man, even a studious man, enjoys the physical pleasures, *n'est-ce pas*? Perhaps the sort an Englishman and his wife do not engage in?"

The veiled reference to fellatio was amusing.

As if to emphasize her willingness to perform the act, she slid her tongue across her upper lip.

Startlingly, Bertram's prick responded favorably. But a tongue was a tongue, right? A mouth, a mouth? Did it matter the gender?

He did nothing when she tugged on the waistband of his trousers. His prick livened even more when she began unbuttoning. Bertram sucked in a sharp breath as the woman knelt before him.

Despite the darkness, Bertram closed his eyes. He could imagine someone else, someone he actually wanted, someone—

The giggle of a woman and the laughter of a man struck Bertram as being far too close. Nearby shrubs jostled.

Good God. Was this some notorious part of the garden where lovers retreated?

In a flash, Bertram's situation came all too clearly into focus. No, it did not matter that the stranger was a woman. But everything else mattered. The intention, the individual, the connection.

Despite his cock desperately needing sensual release, getting sucked off by a stranger behind a shrub was not what his heart and mind wanted.

He stilled the woman's hand as she reached the final button of his fly. "Ah, madam, I am afraid I must decline your generous offer."

As he frantically put his clothing to rights, she stood and offered a sly and knowing smile. "Hmm. Perhaps there is no wife at home. But there is someone who occupies your heart." Her palm hovered over his chest, not touching this time. She nodded her good night and walked away into the night.

The ache in his crotch was from opportunity lost. The ache in his heart was from the misery of impatience for an imagined possibility.

* * * * *

THEY LEFT THE party before midnight. Berrick insisted they ride with him and François and not bother hiring one of the many carriages huddled along the gravel drive to take home weary party-goers.

Percival hesitated. What he really wanted to do was walk. His mind and body still buzzed from the thrill of the party and he needed to expel his nervous energy.

"Please," Berrick said with a wink. "I want to hear all the gossip."

"All right," he agreed. "But only to the *Avenue de la Gare*. It's such a lovely night and I want to exercise my legs." Lady Suffield's was a little too far afield for walking home anyway.

Of course, Berrick and François did all the gossiping since Percival and Bertram were unfamiliar with most of the guests. The ride was like an extension of the excitement of the party.

They were let out above the grand *Place Masséna*.

"Are you certain?" asked Berrick. "It is really not a problem to take you up the hill."

"Thank you," said Percival. "But it's really not so very far for us."

"We're used to traversing the hills of Umbria, remember," added Bertram with a chuckle.

After taking their leave, the two walked side-by-side on the pavement of the mostly empty boulevard. The moon and stars filtered through the canopy of plane trees. Street lamps and muted illumination from a few shops were their guiding lights.

The evening had been unexpectedly enjoyable. Lady Suffield's mansion had been exquisite, and Percival had stolen away not just a few times to study the ancient artifacts displayed in her galleries and public rooms. Her granddaughters Leah and Annette had chatted with him about their lives in England, what they thought about France, what books they had recently read, what games they loved to play, and sometimes about nothing at all.

Every moment had been wondrously captivating.

"A penny for your thoughts, Percy."

Percival glanced up. He'd been abstractedly following Bertram's footfalls. They were already past the train station. "What?"

"You've been silent since we said our good nights to Berrick and François."

"I have?"

Bertram laughed. "Well, from my perspective at least. I can't hear what you're thinking."

Percival chuckled. His head *was* rather full of all his thoughts. "I enjoyed myself at Lady Suffield's, and I had a grand time talking with Leah and Annette."

"I could tell. I don't think I've ever seen you laugh so much."

"They were ever so engaging. But the best part was they did not really know who I was, only that my father was a friend of their grandmother's. I was just another party guest. Someone close to their own age." Percival inhaled the cool night air. "I felt alive. I could be myself, my true self. Not having to play the part of the Duke's heir, or someone's…swain."

Bertram's hand brushed against his before intertwining their fingers then letting go. The brief touch was reassuring. And ever so splendidly arousing.

"Leah—Lady Leah really—is seventeen and to have her debut next year. This summer visiting her grandmother is a diversion during her last year of freedom, as she put it. And when she said such a thing, the look on Annette's face was equally panicked."

"How tragic."

"It really is. Then I think of my own situation and realize the truth she speaks. Marriage is not freedom. It is, as you say, tragic."

"It can be," Bertram said quietly.

Ah, yes. "I did not mean to disparage your parents."

"I think a better way of putting it would be, forced marriages are tragic."

That *was* more accurate. "Indeed."

"And being in a situation where you see no way out of such a tragedy must be thoroughly distressing."

Yes, that was too true.

"I imagine you and Lady Leah found humor as a comfort to your respective impending dooms."

"We did. In a sort of childish way, I suppose. But it was all rather fun." Percival chuckled as he took off his hat to fan his face. "But what about you? Did you meet anyone interesting?"

"Not really." Bertram unbuttoned his waistcoat then flapped it open. "I chatted with Berrick, and a few others. I prefer to observe when I'm among people I don't know." He removed his jacket and hat. "Thank God we're almost home. It's a lovely evening, but not when one is walking up a hill."

Percival unbuttoned his own waistcoat, instantly cooling his heated torso.

Had they been down at the Promenade des Anglais the evening would have been perfect for lovers on a stroll.

"I wish I could hold your hand," Percival murmured.

Bertram emitted a lecherous rumble. "That would be delightful." He shifted his jacket and hat to his other arm. "However, as close friends, we are allowed the next best thing." He wrapped his free arm around Percival's shoulder.

Percival snuggled against him, encircling an arm around Bertram's waist. Even with the humidity in the air, a tingling chill suffused his skin.

They walked as such until they reached the entrance portal of the villa. Inside the foyer, Bertram gave Percival's hand a gentle squeeze. They mounted the dimly lit stairs together to their suite. Once inside the sitting room, Bertram proceeded to the door to his room, but Percival held back.

He locked the door to the sitting room. Bertram turned at the click of the latch.

Percival's heart pounded. "Would you like to join me in my room tonight?"

Bertram dropped his jacket and hat on the floor and, in a few long strides, was before Percival, grinning. "I'd hoped you'd ask.

I'd feared any appeal on my part would have seemed too…presumptuous." He reached out his hands in invitation.

Percival wrapped his arms around Bertram's neck and pulled in for a kiss.

The viscount's enthusiastic growl reverberated through his chest as their lips feasted hungrily. Percival opened his mouth wider and Bertram dived in with his tongue, emitting another growl as Percival sucked him down, pressing their bodies tightly together.

When more air was necessary, they broke apart, panting.

"Let's continue in my room." Percival leaned his forehead against Bertram's.

"Yes, let's."

Hand-in-hand they scurried to the bedroom. Percival shut the door behind them. A whoosh of an exclamation sent him spinning around. Bertram stood at the foot of the bed, staring at the covers.

"What's wrong?"

Bertram pointed. "Er, not wrong, just surprising."

For there at the foot of the bed Armand had placed Bertram's nightshirt and dressing gown alongside Percival's.

Percival laughed in shocked glee. "I suppose it's a subtle invitation for you to feel welcome sleeping here, now we have new servants."

"I would love to." Bertram lifted a brow in query as he grabbed the open front of his waistcoat. At Percival's nod, he proceeded to divest himself of waistcoat, braces, and shirt, the moonlit night casting shadows on the masculine cut of his torso.

Percival stared at the tempting sight, enthralled.

With a wink and a smile, Bertram grappled Percival, taking him in another kiss, this one burning with erotic need.

"Let me pleasure you," he murmured, his voice gravelly, as his fingers skittered up Percival's back to his shoulders.

"Yes, please."

Bertram pulled off Percival's waistcoat and braces then dropped to his knees. "Take off your shirt," he said as he unbuttoned the fly now at eye level.

Percival shivered at the command, in want, not fear. As Bertram tugged down his trousers and drawers, his heart pounded in anticipation not dread.

Warm wetness around the head of his cock sent him lurching forward in momentary disbelief. He gripped Bertram's muscular shoulders, drawing in a thick inhalation, steadying his deliriously spinning senses, as tongue, teeth, and lips took him on a dizzying journey.

Good God, the sensations were indescribable, incomparable. Bertram dug fingers and nails into the flesh of his buttocks, the pain mingling deliciously with the profound pleasure to create sublime rapture. His stones tightened, yearning to release.

Through a lightheaded haze, Percival tried to focus on the consideration being paid to his cock, whirling in a storm of ecstasy, catching a wave of euphoria, riding it higher and higher—

"Fuck."

He spent his seed into Bertram's mouth, still relentlessly sucking, draining him.

Bertram released his hold and Percival collapsed to the carpet.

The viscount was at his side immediately. "Percy, are you all right?"

Percival calmed his breaths as delirium subsided. An acrid smell teased his nostrils. "Is that what it…what I smell like?"

Bertram grinned. "You want to taste it?" He puckered up and leaned in.

"Ugh, no." Percival planted a palm on his chest to hold him back while Bertram laughed.

When amusement subsided, Percival gazed into his lover's eyes, a glimmer of moonlight highlighting the tender emotion within. "I've been greedy letting you pleasure me."

"But I *wanted* to pleasure you. I'm the greedy one."

He, greedy? Is this what it was like to have a lover who was one's equal?

Bertram drew the backs of his fingers across Percival's cheek. "It's all right. We're both tired. And for once we get to sleep in the same bed as we were meant to do. As lovers and friends."

A flush suffused Percival's face. Luckily, the coy reaction would be imperceptible in the dark. "I would like to wake up next to you properly for once."

"That would be lovely, wouldn't it?" Bertram stood and helped Percival up, twisted as he was in his lower garments.

He removed his trousers and drawers. Should he wear his nightshirt? A sudden rush of abashment impelled him to grab it off the bed and put it on. "You don't mind, do you?"

"As long as you don't mind my nudity."

"No." Percival gazed at the now fully undressed body before him. "I rather like you in the nude."

This was met with a smile and a proffered hand to lead him to bed.

"Let me suck you, Bertie. I want to suck you." Desperation edged Percy's plea. He knelt on the carpet and took Bertram's aching erection into his mouth—

A snort jolted Bertram out of his luscious dream. For a panicked moment, he forgot where he was. The window seat was on the wrong side of the room, the moon streaming in through closed curtains when he usually opened his before he went to sleep. Jostling beside him on the mattress roused his memory.

Right. He was in Percival's bed because they could sleep together now. He restrained a chuckle. Maybe this time sharing a bed would be more successful.

And now he was fully awake, his hand wrapped around his unslaked cock.

Bollocks. He couldn't just toss himself off in bed. He'd have to get up.

He stilled, listening to Percival's breathing. The steady rhythm with a slight snore suggested the marquess was fast asleep.

A little thrill pulsed through Bertram's chest. That Percival slept so soundly meant he felt safe with Bertram at his side. But, was the marquess ready to engage in an erotic relationship?

God. He hoped so.

Bertram's pulsed raced. The thought of Percival's mouth around his cock increased the urgency for gratification.

Carefully, silently he lifted the covers from his body then slid one foot onto the rug. Bracing himself, he slipped out of bed.

He grabbed his nightshirt now fallen onto the floor and went to the window seat. He opened the curtain just a little and climbed inside. Through the clear panes of the window the moon and stars were voyeurs to his nude body. He spit on his palm, then stared at the moon and stroked himself, swiftly building to a hasty rhythm.

Ideally, he would linger, thinking about a stranger's warm, wet mouth, preferably that of a handsome man, but the prospect of a seasoned and sophisticated French woman was intriguing. He could only dream that his Percy would ever touch him in that regard. The woman's offer had been real. Had he taken her up on her proposal, he would not be behind a curtain, mocked by the moon, plagued by fantasies of Percival, while the marquess himself slept.

Bertram increased his tempo, his mind now fixated on the locus of pleasure that was his cock. Behind him, Percival snored, the sound a reminder of the object of his affection and his profound desire for him. Too quickly his climax burbled, then rose up like the jet of a fountain, washing over him.

He pressed the collar of his nightshirt against his mouth, muffling his groans, and the hem around his cock, catching his spendings.

Bertram's heart pounded as he descended from his orgasm. Quietly, he emerged from behind the curtain, dropped the nightshirt on the carpet, and crawled into bed beside his beloved.

~ INTERLUDE ~

The Adventures of Paolo the Pirate Hunter, the Magnificent Adventurer, who, along with his First Mate Barnaby, Protects the Seas from the Evil Pirate Jonas the Marauder

by Bertram Atherley, The Right Honorable 2nd Viscount Ravensburgh

Once again, they had failed. Failed to capture the blackguard. Failed in their duty to protect those who needed their help the most.

Barnaby stood on the deck of the *Georgius*, salty, wet wind whipping against his face. He grabbed the pommel of his pistol, stroking the brass butt-cap as his fingers itched to shoot at something, anything.

A gentle hand on his shoulder calmed him. "Patience, Barnaby. Patience. If we wait, the pirate will come to us."

"Yes, Captain." Barnaby let go of his gun. He closed his eyes, centering his attention on Paolo's care-laden touch as he filled his lungs with the bracing sea air.

"We know his course now." Paolo had leaned closer, the heat of his breath fanning across Barnaby's ear. "We will out-maneuver him and capture him when he least expects it."

"Ah, yes, the element of surprise." Barnaby turned, the scabbard of his cutlass crossing Paolo's sword hanging at his hip. He grinned. "You are also prepared for the expected battle."

"I am." He squeezed Barnaby's shoulder. "But I am willing to wait. We can put our time to good use by practicing for the fight." Paolo stepped back and gestured at the deck boards. "Barnaby, dispel your frustration by joining me in a bit of sword-play."

Barnaby's grin grew wider. He took off his jacket and tossed it on the deck. "I would love to practice with you, Captain." He drew his cutlass from its leather scabbard and set his feet apart, his body thrumming in anticipation. "*En garde.*"

With a hearty guffaw, Paolo stripped off his jacket. He pulled out his cutlass with exuberance then held his stance. "May the best man win."

A charge filled the air between them. Who would make the first move?

Barnaby lunged, thrusting his cutlass, the blade instantly deflected by Paolo's elegant parry, his riposte compelling Barnaby to retreat. The captain circled, a smirk curling his lips, his advance slow and steady.

A teasing flick of Paolo's tip caught Barnaby's blade. "I can tell your mind is elsewhere."

Paolo's blade circled around Barnaby's, at times tapping it, a flirtation of steel with steel.

"You should be thinking about the future, not the past. Our victory, not our defeat."

His words resounded like the *ting* of the blades.

"Then I should focus." Barnaby advanced quickly, gliding his blade along Paolo's, gaining leverage for his attack.

But Paolo was too swift, his counter-attack graceful and controlled, his strike against Barnaby's blade almost disarming him, sending him stumbling backwards.

The captain's gleeful yowl rent the air. His eyes blazed with fierce intensity as a scowl of determination hardened his visage. Did he enjoy fencing with Barnaby so very much? Or was he dogged in his quest to rid the seas of the enemy and Barnaby was the proxy?

Barnaby righted himself. "I have this queer feeling you are about to win, my captain."

Paolo lunged, his blade aimed at Barnaby's heart. Barnaby parried, his sharp downward thrust countered with an upward stroke he was barely able to repel.

"Let's try another stratagem." Paolo paced. "Take out your displeasure upon my blade." He held out his cutlass. "As hard as you wish."

Barnaby raised an eyebrow. Paolo nodded and extended his cutlass.

Releasing pent up emotions, Barnaby clashed his blade against Paolo's, the latter's held solid and sturdy, the force of impact ringing through the air and up Barnaby's spine.

"Another," said Paolo.

Barnaby complied.

"Another. As many as you wish."

Barnaby rained blow upon blow on Paolo's blade, each clang depleting his frustrations a little more until his resolve was thoroughly weakened.

"I think there is strength yet in you."

"Perhaps." Barnaby drew in a lungful of air and smashed his blade down. The upward force of Paolo's sword unbalanced him, unwittingly losing his grip, the cutlass skittering across the deck boards.

Paolo seized Barnaby, one strong arm wrapping around his heaving chest, as the tip of the cutlass hovered at his throat.

"You are vanquished, Barnaby Heath."

"I concede to the better man."

"More importantly, you have conquered your frustrations. Let us go forth together to defeat the villain."

"Aye, Captain. I am ready."

~ * ~ * ~ * ~

CHAPTER FIFTEEN

Barnaby slammed down his tankard. Ale could not slake his thirst
while frustration seethed within.
— *The Adventures of Paolo the Pirate Hunter*

Under a wide umbrella, Percival relaxed into the beach chair,
digging his toes into the sand as he lengthened his legs. The sun
seemed more golden, the water more blue, the sand more fine, the
air more fresh. All because he had woken up that morning next to
his fabulously nude best friend.

Bertram sat next to him in a matching chair, reading a book,
wearing dark tinted spectacles he'd purchased from a street vendor
in town. Percival glanced in his direction, gazing at an
exceptionally handsome profile, one that reminded him more of
the cherished childhood chum than the villainous relation.

A chill passed over his flesh. Was that why he hesitated at
times? When his Bertie wanted to be physically close, did he
perceive the family resemblance, the Atherley brown eyes and
hair? And yet, when Bertram kissed him, when he touched him,

there was absolutely no malevolence on the viscount's part. There was only affection, gentleness, and, whenever they were intimate, only gratifying fulfillment.

They'd been sleeping in the same bed the last three nights, each night more erotic than the one before. The night Bertram got on his knees to suck his cock had been a revelation that sex could be a pleasurable experience emotionally, not just physically. The next night, after sharing too much wine, they'd spent kissing, stroking, more kissing, then falling asleep. Last night, they had kissed a little, held each other, and fallen asleep in each other's arms.

Percival glanced over at Bertram again, this time with a smile. If such nights were an indication of their future, then he'd be quite content.

"You keep looking at me." Bertram lifted a brow over his spectacles.

"What are you reading?"

"Really? That's why you keep looking at me?" He sounded disappointed. He turned over the book to look at the cover. "A book of poetry. 'Leaves of Grass' by Walt Whitman. He's American."

"Do you like it?" Percival nibbled on his lip.

"Yes." Bertram smirked, then returned to his book.

Percival gathered courage. "You're incomparably handsome."

The book forgotten, Bertram slid off his chair and rolled over until he lay on the blanket at his side, his face in line with Percival's crotch. He surreptitiously drew a finger along Percival's thigh, sending a tingling thrill up his hip and over to his enlivening cock.

"So that's why you were looking at me." Bertram licked his lips as he ogled the mischief he was causing.

Percival glanced around. They were quite alone. He ruffled his fingers through Bertram's hair, the sensation causing his erection to grow harder.

"Damn," Bertram breathed. "You know how to tease, don't you?" With a flick of his wrist, he tossed his dark spectacles to land on his book. Like a snake, he slithered and arced until they were face to face. "What's for dessert tonight, my lord?"

Desire spiked every nerve of Percival's body. He hardly knew how to respond to such insinuation.

Bertram's mouth curled into a knowing smile. "A surprise, then."

"No, I mean, what would you like?" *Oh, God,* he'd killed the mood, hadn't he?

Bertram's chuckle eased his mind. "Percy, love, I know this is all rather new to you." His gaze dropped to Percival's erection. "But you have desires just like I do—"

Perhaps not *exactly* like his…

"—and I'm willing to explore every single one of them."

Percival swallowed hard. "You're just so much more experienced in these sorts of things. And I'm not at all certain what I want."

"I can help with that." His tone was so seductive.

Percival cupped Bertram's cheek, the scrape of stubble electrifying. "I need to go slowly. What we've done the last few nights has all been rather new to me."

Bertram's smile wilted as if he were crestfallen.

Damn. He needed to rectify the situation. "I really like sleeping with you."

"And I as well, Percy. I just…" Bertram sighed. "The closeness of your body drives me to a frenzy."

"You could toss off while I'm not looking." The moment he said it, he wanted to take it back.

A flush colored Bertram's cheeks, from guilt or frustration he did not know. He huffed a sigh. "I confess I have." He caught his gaze. "It's not the same, Percy. I need to be with you." He stood, his own arousal very apparent. "And now I need to cool off in the water."

Percival watched his lover walk into the sea, arms outstretched, like Christ on the cross.

Or a martyr.

Damn and blast. His Bertie was nothing like Jack, absolutely nothing. But something buried deep in Percival's soul was still preventing his body from moving beyond the past and embracing the possibilities that lay ahead.

He absolutely needed to work to set his soul at ease. His Bertie was his destiny.

ANOTHER LOVELY afternoon at the beach had been another afternoon of abstemious torture.

Bertram reclined on the window seat in Percival's bedroom, wearing one of the marquess's luxurious dressing gowns, the slippery silk sensuous against his naked body. He watched as Percival finished undressing himself after having dismissed Armand.

Simple acts like dismissing a valet were indicative of Percival becoming more sure of himself while he was far away from home. Bertram hoped he would hold on to some of that certitude when confronting the Duke of Amesbury about his future.

"You look deep in thought." Percival tied the sash of his equally luxurious dressing gown and took a place opposite him on the window seat. He extended one leg between Bertram's, his toes tickling along his calves.

"Truthfully? I was thinking about how your dismissing Armand before he had completely undressed you was a tiny sign of your independence."

"My independence?" Percival wriggled his toes again. "How so?"

"That you can undress yourself."

Percival laughed. "I dressed and undressed myself often while at Oxford."

"I never knew that. I thought you always had a valet in tow."

"Armand was my scout then. But the irregularity of my schedule meant he was not always there when I needed to dress for dinner or whatnot."

"A scout?"

"You know the servants who make your bed and sweep your room. Or in my case, I believe Armand hired out all the domestic chores and was just there to lay out my clothes and such." He offered a quizzical look. "Did you not have scouts in Cambridge?"

"Yes, but we called them bedders."

Percival chuckled. "Anyway, I figured out how to dress and undress myself. I can even tie my own four-in-hand knot. I just don't want to all the time. I enjoy being pampered. Armand treats me very well."

"With honor and respect."

Something about those words made Percival blush, then look away out the window. "His small favors and indulgences have worked wonders in helping to heal my mind and spirit."

And Bertram hoped he would be the one to heal his body.

"Being with you has been particularly freeing." Percival tickled Bertram's inner knee with his big toe. "You've done a great deal to help me liberate myself from my past."

The tickling was in earnest now, involving all toes. Bertram grabbed the bedeviling foot. Percival squawked amid laughter, trying to extricate himself in a most ineffectual manner, his jerks and kicks limp and weak. Bertram danced his fingers through the blond hair along the shapely calf.

Percival's eyes were bright with tears of mirth. "Shall we to bed?"

"Oh, yes. Absolutely." Bertram hoped he conveyed sensible anticipation and not the intense lust that was coursing through him.

Percival freed himself from Bertram's forgotten hold and bounded off the window seat. He removed his dressing gown and, as he did every night, draped it over the back of his slipper chair. He then peeled off his nightshirt, revealing his utter nudity, and draped the garment in the same manner.

Bertram swallowed the saliva suddenly pooling in his mouth.

Percival stood with hands on waist, a gentle rock of his hips swinging his stones. "I, too, shall prefer to sleep in the nude tonight."

He went to the bed, and Bertram followed him, dowsing the lamp before inelegantly dropping his dressing gown at the foot of the bed.

Under the covers, Percival slid smoothly inside the cocoon of Bertram's embrace, the lingering scent of ocean teasing his nostrils. The marquess's sculpted abdomen and sleek chest were a delight under his wanton hands, as his engorged cock snuggled in the warmth of the cleft rubbing against it.

Bertram kissed the head, the neck so close to his lips. He closed his eyes, letting his senses of touch, of smell, of taste enliven him. He could be satisfied with just this tonight, really he could.

A jerk against his groin startled him. His eyes now wide in the dark.

The jerking motion became somewhat rhythmic.

Good God. Percival was masturbating, the rocking of his hips rubbing his buttocks along Bertram's cock. He shifted until his shaft stroked the seam of the furred cleft.

Percival's breathy moans were an aphrodisiac to his ears, an accompaniment to the sensual journey on which he was an unexpected traveler. Bertram clung tightly to the body now undulating in his embrace, dragging him down the path toward ecstasy, his cock craving touch, clamoring for release, his conscience counseling him to hold back.

Bertram squeezed his eyes shut against the carnal onslaught, knowing he would not be able to provide relief to the concupiscence churning within. This was Percival's moment. He'd let him revel in it despite his own suffering.

And somewhere deeply buried in that agony he found pure and utter joy.

The cadence of Percival's thrusts quickened until the marquess arced against him with a clipped cry, stiffening for what seemed like a full minute. With a loud sigh he relaxed, slumping into the curve of Bertram's obliging body.

Percival panted as if he had run a race. "I've never done anything like that before."

Masturbate? Surely Jack had allowed him to masturbate? "Like what?"

"Toss off in another man's presence but not for his amusement."

Damn. A chill crept across his scalp. How positively horrifying. Bertram gave him a squeeze. "And how did it feel? I mean, besides the obvious."

A chuckle reverberated against his chest. "It felt freeing. I was in control of my own urges. I could do anything. And at the same time there was a sense of relief, as if a weight had been lifted off my shoulders."

The weight of the past. "That's wonderful, Percy." Bertram nuzzled his nose against his neck and dared to lick the heated flesh.

"Can we do that again sometime?"

Oh, God, yes. "Absolutely."

"Bertie," Percival began hesitantly. "I apologize for ignoring your pleasure tonight."

Bertram chuckled. "Believe me, I felt a great deal of pleasure. Even though I am left ungratified."

He did feel all of that. But he was not entirely telling the truth.

He was grateful his Percy was becoming whole, but how many more nights of this could he endure?

CHAPTER SIXTEEN

Defeating the villain would take time…and patience. But Barnaby
was out of patience. He'd do it without Paolo if he had to.
— *The Adventures of Paolo the Pirate Hunter*

As the hall clock struck four o'clock in the afternoon, Percival sneaked down the stairs to the ground floor. He'd been trying to read a history of the Visigoths in the suite's sitting room with not much luck. He'd been stuck on a single paragraph for what seemed like practically an hour.

He knew exactly why the words danced on the page rather than being absorbed by his brain. Because he missed Bertram.

He'd not seen the viscount since breakfast. As they'd sipped their coffees and read sections of the newspaper, Bertram had announced he wanted to work on his story that day.

"Would you like some company?"

"I'd rather work alone in the library, if you don't mind."

That was hours ago. After breakfast, Percival had walked around the town, looking at sights, watching people, enjoying luncheon with a view of the sea. He even stopped into the public library in the old town which had some objects of antiquity on display. But by the end of the day, despite the amusements, enchanting coastal views, and lovely weather, he felt empty inside.

Because he desperately missed his Bertie.

He needed Bertram. Not in the way he had been bonded to Jack. That had been more like trickery, where Jack would lob threats and ultimatums. No, his craving for Bertram was more akin to feeding one's soul.

Which meant the abrupt way the viscount had left at breakfast had been a blow. As if he *needed* to be alone. Needed to not be with Percival.

And that made him worry.

He hesitated on the stairs. Was Bertram still in the library? Had it been long enough? Had he got his work done as he wanted?

Breaking in on a writer during a time of concentration would surely not put Percival on his good side.

Luckily, Claude exited the library at the very moment Percival arrived at the bottom step.

"Is Viscount Ravensburgh within?"

"*Oui, monsieur le marquis.* He is taking tea."

All right, so Bertram was having a bit of a break at the moment. Percival thanked Claude and knocked on the library door.

A long beat of silence was followed by "enter."

Heart pounding, Percival opened the door to the library.

Bertram sat in an easy chair next to a tea table, a book on his knee. He looked up. "Percy?"

"May I come in?"

"Absolutely. Please do." He motioned to the matching easy chair. "Claude brought tea for two." He chuckled. "I didn't specify how many cups. I suppose he assumed you would be joining me."

So far, Bertram seemed to be in a convivial mood. Percival poured a cup and took a seat.

"I've been home since around three o'clock, so I guess he imagined you and I had made a date for tea."

Bertram tucked his book under his chair and picked up his tea cup. "Did you see some sights today?"

"I did. The usual, you know. The Promenade, monuments, the old town."

"Did you enjoy yourself?"

"I suppose." Percival took a sip of tea. "But, I admit, I was terribly lonely."

Bertram grunted. "I'm sorry to hear that." He put down his tea cup then stood, pacing a little before turning to face Percival.

A crinkle between his eyes was a harbinger of potentially unwelcome news.

"I thought we might spend more time apart during our holiday."

Panic gripped Percival's gut. "Oh?" *Damn.* Was it because—

"I'm sorry I was so utterly selfish last night. I mean about my own pleasure."

Bertram's mouth fell open, as if stunned. "Percy, I didn't mean to imply that," he said softly. "I'm glad you felt comfortable enough to…to do such a thing in my presence. I would never want you to feel anxiety while you pleasure yourself."

"Oh." Percival tried to calm the frantic beating of his heart. "Then why do you want us to be apart?"

"It's about me." Bertram sighed. "I had hoped you…I mean, had hoped we'd have progressed further in our relationship after spending time together. But I realize you're not as ready as I am. So I need to slow down. And to help me slow down, we need to spend some time apart."

But he *was* ready. He really was. At least he thought he was. "Oh."

"And I think we should sleep separately for a while."

Percival's heart felt as if it had been run through with a sword. "You don't want to sleep with me anymore?"

Bertram let out a breath. "I do, believe me I really do. But every night you are by my side is vexatious misery. I wake in the morning on edge and desperate for release."

"But—"

"Yes, you told me, I can go frig myself in solitude."

Tears spiked Percival's eyes. He willed himself not to cry. "Bertie, please understand. I'm not playing games. I am still so reticent and wary. I'm not sure you quite understand what I went through—"

"But I do," Bertram interrupted caustically. Glancing at Percival, he balked, his face softening. "I knew Jack," he said gently. "Knew what he was capable of. I understand completely."

That Bertram knew his cousin was indisputable. But Bertram hadn't lived through the horrors his cousin could inflict.

Percival's heart pounded in his ears, the only noise in the intense silence.

Bertram sat, rubbing his palms along his thighs. "Percy, I am not Jack. I am your friend, and I will always be your friend. But I wish us to be something beyond mere friends. If this is not a situation you can fully accept right now, then I need some time away from you. Your presence is too distracting." His gaze fell on Percival, beseeching. "You understand, right?"

I can do better, was all he wanted to say. But deep in his heart he knew it would take some time. "I understand, Bertie."

Very early the next morning

BERTRAM STOOD IN the middle of his bedroom, the early morning light casting a rosy glow on the carpet bag at his feet. Across the sitting room in the next bedroom, Percival was sleeping, oblivious. Was the marquess sleeping in the nude? Or was he wearing a nightshirt?

Probably snoring.

A chuckle faded into too potent a reminiscence.

Either way, Percival's lithe body was always rousing. And the reason Bertram had to leave.

Percival's surprise act of masturbation the other night had been enthralling, filling Bertram with hope that a new chapter had begun.

But clearly the act had only been a tiny step forward for Percival. It had not been a solid advancement in releasing him from the prison of Jack's restraints.

Percival's reticence lingered. And Bertram wasn't sure he could trust himself to wait for the reluctance to dissipate.

When would Percival be truly ready to fully share his sensual life with another man?

Or, rather, how long would Bertram have to wait?

The waiting had made him emotionally weary. Bertram could never, would never win this battle with a ghost. A vengeful, spiteful, malevolent ghost.

He'd used the day before as practice to see if he could be without Percival. Well, he could, but not without fantasies inundating him. And when Percival had shared tea with him in the afternoon, he'd realized the marquess's presence would foment frustration for the remainder of their holiday.

What he needed was time away from temptation. Time apart from Percival. A little distance between himself and France with its bittersweet memories.

As he'd packed his bag that morning, Bertram recalled he'd contemplated for one moment asking Berrick for a local renter to ease his sexual needs. Then the image of a woman wanting to suck his cock had invaded his brain. That he had been so desperate to have contemplated either disgusted him now, and left him riddled with guilt. Sex with a stranger no longer appealed. Instead, such an act would be pathetic and reprehensible and demeaning to his relationship with Percival.

And would have made him no better than his despicable cousin Jack.

Bertram stared at his carpet bag, the loops and scrolls of the vegetal design on the fabric now blurred. He squeezed his eyes shut, wringing out tears.

If he left today, he'd be in England in three days. He'd write his explanation to Percival once he'd arrived in Hertfordshire.

CHAPTER SEVENTEEN

Despite the warmth of the sun, a breeze off the ocean blew an icy
chill on Paolo's shoulders. Barnaby had gone ashore, leaving him
bereft of his assistance. More than that, the loss of companionship
left him desolate.
— *The Adventures of Paolo the Pirate Hunter*

Later that morning

The night had been restless. Although Percival's opening his
eyes against a sliver of sunlight was proof he had gotten some
sleep the night before.

Some, but not much.

The hall clock struck ten o'clock. *Damn.* He'd wanted to get
up early. Which was probably precisely why he'd had a sleepless
night of worrying he would not get up in time.

He needed to see Bertram after their first night apart. Well,
their first night apart after having been together so many nights.

He jumped from his bed and tugged on his dressing gown, almost ripping a sleeve in his haste, then ran downstairs to the breakfast room.

Empty.

All right. Back upstairs then. He hurtled up the steps two at a time, the forward thrust of his body preventing him from slipping on the vermilion runner.

He knocked on Bertram's door, the slamming of his heart louder than the rap of his knuckles on the wood.

The knob turned, and the door creaked open revealing Claude.

"Ah, *marquis* Norrington. Good morning."

"Good morning, Claude. I'm searching for Viscount Ravensburgh, if he is available." Percival craned his neck to see inside the bedroom.

The bed was made and devoid of an occupant, as it would be at this late hour. The rug, however, was strewn with traveling boxes.

His heart pounded several beats a little too loudly.

Claude smiled dutifully. "Lord Ravensburgh has gone into town to inquire about railway schedules."

A chill of horror stilled Percival. "Oh? Did he happen to mention when he would return?"

"My lord Ravensburgh said if he were to book passage on a late train, he will return to the villa to collect a few of his boxes. But if he is able to book passage immediately, he will send word. If that is the case, I will ship his belongings to England. Although he requested I also inquire if you would be so generous as to transport the rest of his boxes when you return to England?"

"The rest of…" Percival tried to calm the spike in his heartbeat. "What do you mean?"

"Lord Ravensburgh took only a small carpet bag with him when he left this morning."

"Did he give a reason why he was leaving so suddenly?"

"He did not specify."

No, of course not. He would not indulge secrets to a servant.

"Thank you, Claude."

Percival dashed off to his bedroom, tearing the dressing gown from his body in the process, lifting the hem of his nightshirt over his head. There was no time to call for Armand. His day clothes were already laid out for him anyway. With shaking fingers he fumbled with fastening buttons and braces.

He combed his fingers through his hair as he glimpsed in the mirror.

Well, he was presentable enough.

He called for a carriage, and paced on the gravel during the interminable wait.

The driver flashed him a smile and doffed his hat.

"*La gare*," Percival said as he slipped in beside the driver. "*Vite, s'il vous plaît. Il y a une urgence.*" He handed the man a five-franc piece to emphasize that it truly was urgent he hurry to the train station.

The driver nodded as he pocketed the coin. "*Oui, monsieur.*"

They sped over cobblestones, dodging pedestrians, shoppers, street sellers, ignoring oaths and insults.

How long had Bertram been gone? *Damn.* He should have asked Claude. And what time was it now? His pocket watch said just past eleven. Bertram could have left at six in the morning and caught a ten o'clock train.

He could be miles away by now.

The railway station came into view, the entryway teeming with travelers arriving and departing. The carriage slowed as it wended its way through the crowd.

He leaned out the window and grabbed the driver's arm. "*Attends pour moi.*" He waved more money at the man as an incentive to wait for him. The driver nodded.

Percival leaped from the carriage and ran inside the station.

The destination board listed various stations. He needed to look for only one.

Paris. Which would connect to London.

He found the platform.

He ran, barreling through throngs of travelers along the way, again letting vocalized annoyances slide off his back.

Despite valiant efforts, he was too late.

As the train pulled away from the platform dizziness descended, blurring his vision.

Bertram was gone.

Percival sucked in the coal-laced air, smothering the urge to bawl. He wiped away a recalcitrant tear.

Bertie.

His Bertie.

Jesus. He'd been so damn foolish.

He'd never been able to call someone his own before. Jack was never his. Rather, he was Jack's. But Percival had an excellent rapport with Bertram, an intimacy that went deeper than any friendship he'd ever experienced. The two shared the same sense of adventure, plus the same desire for quiet moments along the way.

And surmounting it all they had an attraction that was profoundly tangible and growing increasingly palpable.

Except Percival still had his qualms. Qualms that had sent Bertram away.

He needed to throttle his fears.

A hurried traveler jostled him from his thoughts. Percival slunk back to the entrance where his driver waited for him. He paid the man for his time, and told him to return to the villa. Percival would walk back.

He needed to think about what to do next. Pour his regrets and apologies out into a letter? Ask for a second chance? Such a missive would greet Bertram once he returned to England.

In the meantime, Percival would banish Jack from his memory once and for all, and let Bertram completely into his heart.

CHAPTER EIGHTEEN

The Fate who'd spun his thread of life suddenly twisted it in the
opposite direction. Barnaby's scheme was in knots, and the villain
remained unbound. Only Paolo could untangle his mess.
— *The Adventures of Paolo the Pirate Hunter*

Bertram sat in the pew at the back of Nice's Basilica of
Notre-Dame. Morning sunlight streamed in through the rose
window on the east end, lighting up the altar. After a fitful night,
and not altogether certain he was going to do what he'd planned on
doing, he needed a place to contemplate. Somewhere quiet.
Somewhere no one would think to look for him.

A church was just such a place.

While he'd settled the bill at the small hotel where he'd spent
the night, the hotelier happened to mention *"notre nouveau
église"*—our new church—built only ten years prior in the neo-
Gothic style. The edifice was near the train station.

The next train to Paris was in a few hours. He would have
time to sort out his riot of emotions in a serene space. He'd even

pretend to pray if he had to, then move along to the train station if that was what he decided to do.

Bertram stared at the carpet bag at his feet. He really didn't want to go back to England. The notion simply seemed like the only way to ease his tortured body and brain.

He lifted his gaze to the altar. The cool, dark, quiet space would certainly be a haven for tourists on hot afternoons. As it was still early in the morning, he was practically alone. A few old women lit candles and knelt before altars in the side chapels, their whispered prayers echoing between slender columns.

Morning in a church was the perfect time for one to be alone with one's thoughts, whatever they might be.

And Bertram's thoughts were entirely of Percival. He could not get the marquess out of his head.

Really he should be thinking about how he was going to pass his time when he returned home. Perhaps visit Nicholas in London and attend a few of the Season's soirées?

But such affairs would be dreadfully boring without Percival at his side.

Which was precisely why Bertram had not had the courage to leave Nice the day before. He'd given himself one night to consider what he was about to do, one night in a hotel alone.

He'd been alone frequently in his life, but he'd never felt lonely. Last night was, simply put, oppressively lonely.

The clang of metal against metal stirred Bertram from his morose thoughts. On the dais of the main altar a gray-haired priest holding a smoking censer busied about. He placed the censer on the dais and adjusted the altar cloth before descending the steps to the aisle.

He walked down the aisle slowly, as if he himself were mired in morning contemplation. Only when he was a few pews away did he notice Bertram.

"*Bonjour,*" the priest greeted with a smile.

"*Bonjour.*" Bertram smiled back.

Gray eyebrows rose in inquisitiveness. "*Anglais*?" He shook his head. "You are English?"

"*Oui*," Bertram responded in kind. "Yes."

"Welcome to the church of Our Lady." He gestured broadly. "We are very proud of our French history."

The neo-Gothic architecture was indeed an homage to ancient France in a town that only twenty years prior been part of the Kingdom of Sardinia. "The basilica is very beautiful."

"The English helped fund our church, and for that we are grateful." His accent was slight, as if he had spent some time in England. He shuffled a little along the aisle. "Will you be visiting Nice for long?"

"I have already been here for over a week."

"Ah." The priest eyed him. "If I may offer an observation?"

"By all means."

"You do not seem as if you have enjoyed your stay here."

Bertram's initial shock twisted into a smile. "Yes, that is an astute observation."

The priest indicated the pew where Bertram sat. "May I?"

"Absolutely." Bertram scooted over. His train did not leave for hours. Talking to a discerning priest might be diverting.

With a labored squat accompanied by a slight grunt, the priest took his place at Bertram's side. "Now, tell me what troubles you."

"There is someone in my life. Someone here in Nice. Our time together has had its frustrations."

The priest nodded. "A lover."

Bertram stared at the man, stunned by his perspicaciousness. But of course, he must encounter the lovelorn and provide counsel in such a romantic place. "Yes." Well, in a sense they were lovers. Sort of.

"And you thought to leave?"

"I've spent the night thinking."

"And what is the essence of the problem?"

Lying to a priest was unnerving. But trying to explain the truth would be risky. "My…friend and I have formed an attachment, but there is an impediment having to do with a trauma in the past. My friend seems unable to heal. I have waited all I can." The threat of tears burned Bertram's eyes. "I think."

"And do you love your friend?"

"So very much."

From within his voluminous habit, the priest retrieved a prayer book. "Do you know your Bible, my son? Corinthians?"

The plaques over the doors of the bedrooms in the villa had been quotes from Corinthians.

"A little. I recently saw an inscription."

"And what did it say?"

"*La charité est patiente, elle est douce.*"

"*La charité n'est point envieuse,*" the priest continued the verse. "And what does this mean?"

"Charity is patient and gentle, is not envious."

The priest nodded. "But what is meant by charity?"

Bertram was struck by the question. "Well, I don't completely recall my boyhood Bible studies, but recently seeing the inscription has made me think a little on it. Perhaps it means an act of charity is a good in its simplicity and purity."

The priest smiled thoughtfully. "We use the word 'charity', but it is an inexact translation. The original Greek word is *agape*."

"*Agape?*" That was the word Percival had used at the Etruscan tomb. "Isn't that a feast of some sort?"

"Ah, so you have heard the word." The priest's face crinkled with enthusiasm. "There was indeed a feast celebrated by the early Christians called *agape*. It was the Eucharistic celebration of the divine love of God. But 'feast' is not the meaning of the word. We have no exact equivalent in our languages, in English or in French. We have usually equated it with charity for a few reasons. One reason is that our early church father St. Jerome had himself a difficult time translating the Greek word, so he chose the Latin *caritas*."

"Which translates to charity in English."

"You have studied your Latin." The priest nodded his approval. "Very good."

Bertram smiled through his flush of bashfulness.

"This translation works, as charity—or an act of charity—displays an unselfishness that compels a man, or a woman," the priest glanced at Bertram, "to give of themselves. But 'charity' does not encompass the divine aspect of *agape*. So, as Biblical scholars delve into translation and clarification, they have begun to settle on a more inclusive term: the word love."

Love? "That seems to change the whole meaning of the verse."

"How so?"

"*Love* is patient? *Love* is gentle? *Love* is not envious? When I think of love I think of an emotion. When I think of charity I think of an act."

There was that enigmatic smile again. "Ah, but is not being patient with someone an act of love? Likewise, when you are kind to them? These are acts. And they show love."

Bertram narrowed his gaze. "But did the apostle Paul truly mean a lover's love?"

The priest laughed. "You are an excellent student, my boy." His expression sobered to thoughtfulness. "I believe Paul meant divine love, the love we should have for God, the love He has for us. But as we are created in His image, it is also the love we have for each other. Love in all its permutations: the love of a mother for her child, the love between friends, perhaps even the love we feel for our vocations and avocations." The priest's smile widened. "But it also includes the love for one's lover. All love, genuinely given, is divine love."

Bertram swallowed the emotion welling in his throat.

"What else does Paul say?" The priest thumped the leather cover of his Bible with his index finger. "He says throughout our lives three divine graces persist: faith, hope, and love. What is Paul's conclusion of this?"

"That the greatest of these is love." Bertram sighed. "But I will need faith and hope to fortify my heart."

The priest patted his knee. "You are such an intelligent young man. You will succeed in your endeavor. You will see."

"You know a lot about love."

The old face crinkled with glee. "I have performed a great many weddings and have counseled a great many couples beforehand. Marriage is a sacrament in the Catholic Church."

"I think it is as such in the Church of England, as well."

The priest nodded. "Yes. Because love is important in the eyes of God. Sometimes I think love is the foundation for all else." He steadied himself as he rose. "I see you have packed your bag." He pointed at the carpet bag with a tremulous finger. "But perhaps you will think about your situation. You are welcome to stay in this house of God for as long as you need. And—" he gripped the back of the pew as he straightened, "I am *Père* Gaspard. Father Gaspard. I am the curate of Notre-Dame. If you decide to stay in Nice, I am here to listen."

Father Gaspard then continued on his way down the aisle, the echo of a heavy door signaling he had exited the basilica.

Bertram stared blankly at the prayer book left on the seat next to him.

Love is patient.

But was he?

Percival stared at the sun-drenched view of the Mediterranean, pen in hand poised over the cotton bond paper perfectly aligned on the portable desk before him. The creamy sheet contained only three words.

My dearest Bertie.

He'd gotten no further than that. His thoughts rattled around in his head, confused, erratic.

He shouldn't be writing a damn letter. He should be on a train following Bertram.

Except all will to move had left his body. After returning from the railway station yesterday, he had done nothing but mope. Last night's supper had consisted of a morsel of food and a bottle of wine. Armand had rousted him from the sofa in the drawing room and hauled him off to bed.

Then regret had woken him up far too early in the morning.

So here he was, having coffee on the terrace at an hour of the morning he usually spent in bed. But he couldn't sleep despite the weariness that weighed him down.

A letter seemed the best means of communicating his feelings, or, perhaps, easing some of the regret of not following Bertram. A letter would arrive in England before he could anyway.

He'd never kept a journal, never felt compelled to write down his thoughts and fears, even when they plagued him after…well, just "after". But through his time at Oxford, Bertram had written him constantly, inspiring Percival to respond. Usually it was to send back the pages of the story Bertram had written marked up with his comments and praise.

To start from a blank page and pour his soul out was positively daunting. He'd rather have Bertram right here before him so he could tell him how he felt with spoken words.

But if Bertram were present, there would be no reason to write a letter, no reason to confess all his feelings because Bertram would have had no reason to leave.

And that, precisely, was the problem, wasn't it? Percival had never truly confessed his feelings. And now he'd lost the best friend and, yes, lover, he'd ever had.

A tear slid down his cheek. He wiped it away before it could mar the practically blank page.

Behind him the terrace door opened and closed. Probably a servant bringing more coffee. He had long finished the first round.

A finely gilded white porcelain coffee pot was placed gently on the micro-mosaic table, and a matching coffee cup and saucer placed alongside.

"Thank you," Percival mumbled as he stared abstractedly at the hands performing the simple tasks.

The very familiar masculine hands.

Percival stood as realization shot through him. The pen dropped onto the terrace flagstones.

"Bertie."

Before him stood Bertram, still wearing his traveling clothes. An air of dishevelment marred his appearance—the shadow of stubble, his jacket a bit rumpled, and a hint of distress on his countenance.

Bertram offered a weak smile. "You look as if you've seen a ghost."

"Forgive me, but I am not certain if this is a dream and you merely an apparition."

"It is truly I before you." His voice held a tremble.

"I thought you in Paris by now." Percival's heart pounded at a dizzying pace.

Bertram stepped forward, then halted. "May I greet you with an embrace?" His bloodshot eyes were limned with damp lashes.

"Oh, God, yes. Please."

They fell into each other's arms. Emotion swelled within until Percival could hold back no longer. He let loose his tears, his body shaking.

Bertram held him more tightly as if to stop himself from shaking, too.

They clung to each other until their shuddering breaths calmed. Percival pulled back a little, then rested his forehead against Bertram's.

"I fear I have left your shoulder sodden with my bawling."

Bertram chuckled as he grabbed his handkerchief from his jacket pocket. "I am guilty of the same."

Percival sucked in air, trying to regain composure. He squeezed his lids together to stem the tide of emotion, but the weighty puffiness of his swollen eyes could not bank a deluge of tears.

Bertram drew in a long inhalation, releasing it slowly. "Percy," he intoned, his voice soft and lulling. "I tried for one day to live without you, and found I could not."

Percival's chest gripped. The tears fell again.

"Yesterday, when I got to the railway station, I couldn't do it. I couldn't leave you." Bertram drew back a little and looked Percival in the eye. "But I had to have some time away to think. So I stayed at a hotel in town."

"I had feared the worst." He still feared it. "That you had left me."

"I know," he admitted. "I mean, I thought you might." He placed his hands firmly on Percival's shoulders. "I am so sorry to have caused you distress. Even for a moment. I should never have left. And I never, ever want to be a source of pain for you."

The anguish in Bertram's voice, palpable and sincere, unleashed yet more tears. Bertram offered him a handkerchief. The embroidered *A* for Atherley should have caused further distress, but it did not.

Something had already changed within, a new strength had been found.

"Thank you." He took the linen square and wiped his eyes.

Bertram pulled out a chair and lifted a brow. "May I join you?"

"Yes. Please." Percival slumped into his own seat.

He stared at his cup while Bertram refilled it, then poured coffee for himself adding a generous pour of milk.

Bertram sipped his brew, his brow knitted in some thought. He sat back, carefully resting the porcelain cup on its saucer. "Do you want to know the real reason I never left England? Never took my own grand tour? I could easily have ventured off to meet up with Nicholas. He'd even invited me to join him. But I didn't. It wasn't the money, or lack thereof, or even that my mother needed me to take care of her. Despite Papa having died overseas, she encouraged travel. But I stayed home." He looked into the distance. "I was waiting for Jack to die." He exhaled then met Percival's gaze. "There, I've said it. He was so damned reckless, I knew he would succumb to some mischief sooner rather than later. And when it would happen, I wanted to be there for you. I wanted a chance to win your heart."

Thank God for the extra handkerchief. Percival dabbed his eyes. "I daresay you have succeeded."

Bertram's grin did not reach his eyes, wherein still glittered some pain. "I was being selfish, Percy. I want gratification upon demand. It's how I've always been with the sensual part of my life. But you're different and you're challenging my habits."

"I can change."

"And so can I." Bertram clapped his hand against the table top. "In fact, it is I who should be the one to change in this relationship. You've been hurt. Badly so. Despite my knowing some of what you went through, I cannot truly comprehend it. I am the one who needs to learn patience."

Bertram reached his hand palm up on the table, over the mosaic scene of lovers waving goodbye along a port.

Or were they lovers reuniting?

"Percy, I am tormented by desire for you. But my torments are nothing compared to the scourge of your own demons."

Percival pressed his palm to Bertram's. "It is time I begin to forget in earnest."

Bertram smiled, his eyes glistening. A tear formed on his lashes. He looked away as he wiped his face. "What's that?"

He grabbed the piece of paper and read the salutation. The smile widened. "You didn't get very far, did you?"

"Apparently, neither did you."

Bertram laughed. "I feel an urge to do something diverting today. I've missed spending time with you."

"We've only been parted a day."

"I know. And yet there is a gnawing emptiness within I must fill with your presence."

Percival's heart swelled before it performed a somersault. "There is a street in the old town where painters sell their wares. I would like to purchase a canvas commemorating our time spent in this lovely town."

"I would greatly enjoy that," said Bertram.

A picture Percival would be able to gaze upon for years, whether or not Bertram was still in his life.

~ INTERLUDE ~

The Adventures of Paolo the Pirate Hunter, the Magnificent Adventurer, who, along with his First Mate Barnaby, Protects the Seas from the Evil Pirate Jonas the Marauder

by Bertram Atherley, The Right Honorable 2nd Viscount Ravensburgh

Like fingers stretching into the sea, two rocky peninsulas extended into the water to form a hidden cove within which the *Georgius* sheltered.

A perfect place from which to launch an attack on Jonas the Marauder.

Ever since the debacle at Nassau Town, the pirate had been two steps ahead of them. But not this time. Paolo had gathered intelligence from townsfolk and mariners about where the pirate was squatting. And Paolo was determined to capture him once and for all.

Spanish Town—the capital of the former pirate stronghold Jamaica, but now much tamed by British occupation—surely would prove to be a superlative location to capture the villain.

Their mooring was private, positioned near beaches. Their path to town would be uncomplicated by such features as high cliffs, but would still be quite an expedition. Paolo and Barnaby, along with their trustworthy and devoted crew, would have to cross miles of treacherous landscape until they reached the town. Every step would be worth it if the villain were vanquished.

A light breeze drifted across the deck where Paolo and Barnaby observed their men maneuvering supplies to the shore.

"We will win," said Paolo.

"We have to," Barnaby declared. "If we are to rid mankind of a scoundrel once and for all."

CHAPTER NINETEEN

"I could've killed him. Shot him. Strangled him. Stabbed him."
Paolo placed a hand on Barnaby's shoulder. "Let the hangman
work his trade. We will remain vigilant as need be."
— *The Adventures of Paolo the Pirate Hunter*

*K*issing.

Bertram had never really kissed much in the past. Well, he
had, but really just as a bothersome prelude to a more lascivious
act. He'd never really mashed as just a prelude to, well, more
mashing.

Until Percival, that was, and his obsession with the simple act
of kissing. Which, as they both got better at it, became a little less
simple and more creative.

Like the other night when Bertram had leaned his head back
on the sofa and Percival had kissed him upside down. The
sensations had been quite unique, and very satisfying, despite both
of them laughing during the first part, until they mastered the act.

Why had it taken him so damn long to discover kissing?

Bertram kept his amusement to himself as he sat beside Percival under a couple of umbrellas at their favorite beach. His mind had wandered while he reviewed pages of *The Adventures of Paolo the Pirate Hunter*. Luckily, the dark spectacles shielded his furtive glances from his companion, as well as dulling the glare from the white pages of his notebook.

But last night the kissing had led to something more. As they'd lay side by side in bed, each had pleasured himself, laughing as they raced to orgasm. The winner would be he who spent first. As Bertram worked his cock, he knew he was doomed to lose. He had tossed himself off that very afternoon. And while Bertram was still in the vigor of youth, Percival was at that very excitable age when culmination was too easy. Percival won amidst guffaws and crows of victory.

Bertram dug his toes into the hot sand to distract his enlivening prick from reviving too much from the memory.

"I should be bored," announced Percival. "Any yet, lying on the beach in a torpid state is positively exhilarating." He raised his head. "You should try it. You often spend our beach time working."

Bertram laughed. "I enjoy writing and you inspire me. Although I do admit I also enjoy simply watching you doze."

"I don't snore on the beach, you know."

"You don't, that I can assure you."

Percival snorted. "Pray tell, what are you working on?"

"I'm reviewing the ending of *Paolo*."

"To send to a publisher?"

"Do you think I should?"

"Oh, definitely."

"Then yes." Although Percival might feel otherwise if he knew the truth. He should really tell him, especially with their new intimacy. "I do have you to thank for the story in the first place."

Percival raised himself on his elbows. "Me? How so?"

"You used to make up pirate stories when you were a boy. You used to tell me and Nicky all sorts of stories while we walked the grounds of Atherley Manor."

"I did?" A thoughtful pause. "I remember stories about fairies. Perhaps pirates, but I don't remember pirate hunters." He plopped his head back down on a pillow of sand. "I admit I don't remember much…you know…before…"

A twinge of remorse for bringing up the topic bedeviled Bertram. "You were an innocent, lovely boy. And your enthusiasm for your fantastical stories was rather endearing."

Percival grunted. "I definitely do recall running about the unkempt land. I suppose I spouted whatever came to mind in that untamed state."

"You had me enthralled. Your utter enjoyment of childhood was mesmerizing to me."

"You never had a proper boyhood, did you? You had to be a man too soon."

He did. Papa had died when both of them had been so young. "Not one where I could aimlessly wander along the rolling hills and rocky outcrops of the countryside thinking up outlandish stories. I suppose I envied you at the time. The stories always stayed with me. Even when I read literature at Cambridge. Then, when you were sent away after…what happened, I began thinking about you again. About your stories. So I wrote them to you."

Percival blew out a breath. "I never made the connection. I just thought you were an aspiring writer wanting a friendly reader."

"But I took liberties with the original. You used to play the part of a pirate, wielding sticks as swords and even threatening me and Nicky with rocks as cannonballs."

"I did not."

"Oh, but you did." Bertram laughed, then quickly quieted. "Percy, did you know I based Paolo on you?"

"Me? I'm Paolo? I thought I was a pirate?"

That brought amusement to soften Bertram's apprehension. "When I found out, I was so angry at Jack for what he did to you. I was angry at myself for not knowing the depths of his debauchery, for not looking after you. I guess the story of Paolo and Barnaby conquering evil was a way for me to come to terms with everything that happened. And a way for me to let you know I was there for you if you needed me."

"If Paolo is me, then Barnaby is you?" Percival shook his head with a laugh. "Percival and Bertram. Which means the pirate Jonas is Jack."

"Yes."

Still propped on his elbows, Percival stared at his feet, his too long silence unsettling.

"Percy," he began gently, "I understand if you do not want me to continue revising the story. I'll tuck it away. I can write about Paolo the Etruscan treasure hunter, instead."

Percival shifted to sitting cross-legged on the beach blanket, his hands gripping his knees. "Paolo captures the pirate Jonas does he not?"

"He does."

"And brings him to justice?"

"Yes."

"Then Jonas is hanged."

"He is."

Percival leaned back on his hands. "I want him to be shot instead. I want Paolo to shoot Jonas."

The hairs at Bertram's nape stood on end. He understood completely. "All right." But how to write such a scene? "Let's say one of Jonas's men shoots through the hanging rope and Jonas tries to escape. Paolo subdues the accomplice pirate, then pursues Jonas, all the while warning the crowd to make way. He then shoots Jonas in the back—"

"No," Percival interrupted. "In the front, while their eyes are locked."

"All right, Paolo is able to overtake Jonas because the pirate's hands are still tied behind him—"

"Ooh, excellent detail."

Bertram chuckled. "So Paolo stands before Jonas." He turned to Percival. "Should he make some sort of speech?"

"Hasn't he already? Just get it over with."

"Good. Paolo shoots Jonas dead, and Barnaby comes forward with the accomplice pirate. Hmmm. I'll make it so he was already in prison awaiting being hanged, but then he escaped. He can be hanged on the spot."

Percival smiled. "Sounds like a rather exciting ending. A fine adventure story. I really do think you should get it published." He stretched out once again on the blanket and closed his eyes. "I'm suddenly in the mood for a nap."

Bertram returned to his notebook, scribbling notes for the new plot as fast as he could. The crash of waves and the caws of sea birds were an inspiring accompaniment to a story set on a faraway island.

A tickling touch on his thigh sent a tingling thrill across his flesh. He lifted his spectacles. Percival smiled at him as he drew his fingers along his leg.

"I like what we did last night."

Bertram scowled playfully. "Only because you won."

"Well, yes, that is true. If you haven't yet frigged yourself surreptitiously today, you might have a chance at victory tonight."

Was he really suggesting they play the game again? Hope expanded Bertram's chest. "I have been rather abstemious today. I dare say I shall best you."

Percival laughed. "I thought I might take one more swim before we leave. Care to join me?" He lifted a brow as if to suggest there might be more than just swimming going on in the sea.

If Percival continued to touch him like that, to look at him like that, he'd need a dip in the water to cool his ardor. He stilled the questing hand.

"Yes, let's."

That Percival still desired their friendship even after confessing the secret he'd held so long was heartening.

THE LETTER IN Percival's hand had been read and reread until the words were just a blur yet he'd retained nothing. Sitting across from him on the terrace was the source of his distraction. Bertram was truly engrossed in whatever correspondence he had received from England. His changing expressions reflected the content of the letters, most of which appeared to be amusing or satisfactory news.

Yesterday afternoon, they had dared touch each other under the waves, exciting each other, keeping each other on tenterhooks by cupping each other's pricks, grabbing each other's bums, tangling legs as flapping arms kept them afloat. Such playfulness in the sea always left Percival roused sensually. The last few nights, that playfulness had led to kissing, then more kissing, then mutual masturbation. All of that had subdued his ardor. But now he wanted more. Needed more.

Earlier in their travels, his desires had been hampered by fear. Fear of rejection, fear of dredging up ghosts brought on by memories, fear Bertram would demand too much too soon.

Now he was filled with excited anticipation for what two lovers might do. Poor Bertie, who'd had to put up with all that kissing and his own hand almost every night since his return.

At least he had resumed sleeping in Percival's bed.

The delicate ping of a tea cup against its saucer took him back to the present. He still held the letter from Father. There was one from Mother unopened on the silver salver. Bertram's post seemed far more interesting.

"What news from England, Bertie?"

A smile revealed the contents. "Ah, it seems my mother is faring quite well without me." He searched the letter with his finger. "Here, 'Gretta has been staying over at the house. We've been keeping up your garden. Such a wonderful pastime.'" He turned to Percival. "Margaretta Burnley, otherwise known as Gretta, is a widow who lives in town. She and my mother have been best friends for as long as I can remember. I'm glad she has companionship while I'm gone." He poured himself a cup of tea, looked at Percival's untouched cup, and put the pot down.

"Shall I call for a fresh pot, my lord?"

Percival downed the cold contents of his cup with a scowl. "Please."

Bertram went inside momentarily to ring the bell pull. He returned, then sat and folded the letter from the Viscountess Ravensburgh.

"And the other letter? Is that from Nicky?"

"It is."

"And?"

"He says he's in desperately love with an American heiress and determined to win her hand."

"Let's hope congratulations will be in order, then," he said flatly.

"You don't sound too enthused for my cousin."

Percival sighed heavily. "I am simply not enthused for my own doom with regards to marriage." He brandished Father's letter in the air. "My father the duke inquires about my time spent with Lady Leah and Lady Annette. He apparently received word from some relation of theirs that we had met at Lady Suffield's. He asks whether I enjoyed my time with them." He blew out exasperation, then met Bertram's gaze. "I am only just becoming comfortable with discovering you. Now I have to contend with the prospect of marrying a woman? Ugh. The idea disgusts me."

"Speaking of women, and Lady Suffield's soirée…" A blush colored Bertram's cheeks. "I… well, I…" He inhaled deeply. "I wanted to let you know I was propositioned by a woman at the event."

"Who was she?"

"I don't know. Only that she was a mature confident French woman."

Percival eyed him. "What do you mean by propositioned?"

Bertram took a gulp of tea. "She made it very clear she would perform fellatio if that was my wish."

Good God. "And what did you do?"

"I…" Bertram sighed as he glanced away. "Percy, I have to admit I almost let her do it. I needed to tell you the truth."

"But you didn't go through with it?"

"No. I declined her offer."

So many thoughts bombarded Percival's brain. "Because of me? I mean, you almost took her up on her offer because of me? And you declined her offer because of me?"

"You've hit the mark with that analysis." Bertram's lashes were damp. "But please know I am devoted to us."

"Would you really have let a woman do such a thing to you?"

"The idea of a woman performing such an act on my person is not as repulsive to me as it is to you. To my mind, a mouth is a mouth."

"Good God." This time Percival voiced the oath out loud. "I'm not sure I will ever see your point of view on the matter."

"You're not jealous?"

Percival thinned his lips. He glanced at Bertram, then away. "Despite all the infidelities I had to endure, I was not myself allowed to ever be jealous."

"How—" Bertram stared at him, paling as realization descended. "Percy, oh God, I'm so sorry."

"Nothing really to be concerned about any longer, is it? And now I have an utter lack of such emotion. Perhaps this is a good thing? I don't know. I do know it was perceived jealousy that destroyed the Earl and Countess of St. Albans and their libertine son." He swallowed the lump in his throat. "I was never to blame."

"You were very definitely never to blame. And I apologize for my imprudence."

"I forgive you." He once again met Bertram's gaze. "You miss it, don't you?"

"Miss what?"

"Fellatio."

Bertram heaved a sigh. "Percy, I will not lie to you. I do miss the act. But please know that it is not more important to me than you are. I can wait until you are ready. I mean this."

Percival held out his hand, palm up, on the mosaic table. Bertram grasped his hand.

"Bertie, I think I am ready for something beyond kissing."

CHAPTER TWENTY

When a task is finished—and done well—there is a feeling of great
pleasure.
— *The Adventures of Paolo the Pirate Hunter*

Making love in the middle of the day was not something
Bertram had ever expected so soon after he'd decided to stay in
Nice. But here they were in Percival's bed, lying naked with arms
and legs tangled together. The windows were open but the sheer
inner curtains were drawn to temper the breeze and shade the room
from the afternoon sun.

From the moment Percival had taken off his clothes, Bertram
had had a stiff stander. Percival's erection now pressed into his
thigh, keeping Bertram in his state of arousal. Since Percival had
suggested the tryst, he should be the one make the first sensual
move.

"I really enjoy being with you, Bertie."

"And I, you."

Temptation egged him on, while anticipation held him in check. The mystery of whatever Percival had planned was eating away at him.

"I could stay like this forever, Bertie. In your arms, I mean. You make me feel safe."

Of course, that was exactly how he wanted Percival to feel, but not now. At this very moment, he'd much prefer his Percy to want a bit of danger while in his arms. "I'm glad you want to be with me."

Percival shifted, his lips grazing Bertram's jaw as his tongue drew a wet line. He planted a tender peck on Bertram's cheek, then another, and another until Bertram turned to meet his mouth. As their tongues languidly entwined, Bertram's cock protested against Percival's hip.

That elicited a giggle. "You want more than a kiss, don't you?" Percival said in a teasing tone.

Bertram dared stroke Percival's back, taking in the curve of his buttocks. "You know I do. I always do."

Percival raised himself on an elbow, and traced the curls of the hair on Bertram's chest. "I want this to be right. You've been so patient with me. It's just that…I'm unsure how to proceed. I don't know how other men do this without, you know, the…"

He didn't finish the sentence. He didn't have to. Violence, bullying, berating. Any of those words would have filled in the unspoken emotion.

So nothing that reeked of dominance. Bertram would have to approach this delicately, although his prick wanted anything but delicate.

He met Percival's gaze. "You know there are ways for us to pleasure each other mutually. At the same time, I mean."

A tiny crease of dubiousness formed on the bridge between those gorgeous blue eyes. "Besides lying side by side which we have already been doing?"

"Yes." Bertram could not contain his enthusiasm. "Shall I tell you about them?"

A gentle twitch tugged up one eyebrow. "I'm listening."

"There are two acts I can think of right now, although I'm certain there are more."

That tugged the luscious lips into a smile.

Which act to describe first? Perhaps the one where they would be utter equals. "One act entails each of us pleasuring the other at the same moment. The downside is that sometimes one loses one's sensibilities in the throes of ecstasy thereby forgetting to attend properly to the other."

"Oh, now we can't have that, can we?"

Bertram chuckled. "In the other act, one of us guides the pleasure for both, but the pleasure takes place at the same time."

"How intriguing." Percival danced fingers on Bertram's chest. "Can you go into more detail? For both?"

"In the first act, we lie next to each other topsy-turvy, my head at your groin, your head at my groin, and we pleasure each other with our mouths."

A flash of intrigue momentarily flushed the marquess's cheeks. "You mean I take your cock in my mouth?"

"And I, yours. Then we suck. Or lick, or tease with nibbles." *Fuck*, his cock was iron hard.

"So far I like it." Something akin to mischievousness flickered across Percival's face. "And what's the other act?"

Bertram cleared his throat. "Well, we sit in such a way that our pricks are standing stiff right next to each other. Then one of us takes both pricks in hand and frigs."

Percival emitted a choke of amusement. "One hand around two pricks?" He flexed his fingers wide, examining the span. "Hold up your hand against mine."

Bertram did as directed.

Percival pressed their hands together, then considered the display.

"Our little fingers are about the same size," he said thoughtfully. "But your middle finger and thumb are much thicker." He flashed a smile in Bertram's direction. A blush colored his cheeks as he quickly resumed his study of their hands.

He seemed quite intrigued by the latter option. "Percy, if neither of these suggestions tantalizes, I'm sure I can come up with another idea."

"Oh, no," Percival said quickly as he licked his lips, still staring at Bertram's hand. "I think I like the idea of you frigging us both."

"I?"

"Of course. You have the larger hand." A devious smirk played upon Percival's lips. "And I'll get to watch."

"All right, my lord." Bertram scrambled up to kneel on the bed. "Sit with your legs spread wide and we'll begin."

PERCIVAL MOVED TO the center of the bed and spread open his legs. Bertram faced him and sat similarly, sliding his legs under Percival's thighs, inching his buttocks forward until they were close. Very close. So close the tips of their noses practically touched. That was something of a deflection from the fact their stones were actually touching. Like sentinels, their erections waited, at attention.

Bertram studied their cocks, then flexed his right hand as if measuring his grasp. He gathered both, his palm and fingers easily encircling their girth.

Warmth and a soft hardness urged a growl from Percival's throat, while droplets of arousal seeped from both crowns.

"Good," Bertram said, his voice ragged. "This will help lubricate my endeavor."

He rubbed the fluid across both heads, sending a shiver of excitement through Percival. Already the act was more than he could have imagined.

Bertram released their cocks and spit on his hand. "We'll need more, though."

With one corner of his mouth upturned and an eyebrow arched seductively, Bertram reclaimed both cocks and gave a squeeze. He slid his hand up, then slid his hand down, repeating the act at an excruciatingly slow pace.

The even rhythm was lulling, yet every stroke induced a shudder of anticipation. Percival leaned back on his hands and watched Bertram's ministrations, his mind hypnotized by the movement, his body stimulated by the sensations.

The rhythm increased, but only slightly. Had Percival been under the direction of his own hand, the impatience of lust would have impelled him forward. Each stroke by another man's hand procured apprehension and anticipation whether and when the act would eventually culminate.

He had to trust his lover. And his Bertie was a lover he could trust.

Urgency ultimately impelled Bertram to increase the pace. Percival's balls tightened, each persistent pump bringing him closer to the edge. He continued to watch the erotic act, now through half-lidded eyes and a dazed mind.

Bertram's sharp gasp dragged him out of his erotic stupor. The viscount's mouth hung open, his brown eyes glazed over, signs he was almost at his climax.

He faltered a moment, losing the rhythm, emitting a grunt of despair. After a breath, he resumed his labors, now at a frantic, erratic pace. His countenance twisted and contorted with effort, the muscles of his arms corded with tension as he worked to bring them both off.

Desire mingled with appreciation to incite bravery. Percival grabbed Bertram's wrist, tugging until he released their cocks. He pushed a stunned Bertram onto his back, then swung around and straddled his chest, the viscount's cock standing before his gaze. He leaned over.

The head of his lover's fully engorged cock was poised at his mouth, the smooth purplish-red tip inviting, enticing. He never liked performing the act, hated it, actually. But now he was utterly driven, his mouth salivating, his own cock hardening at the thought of sucking Bertram off.

He wrapped his lips around the glorious shaft, drawing it deep into his mouth.

A litany of oaths spewed forth from Bertram, the humid heat of his breath teasing Percival's balls

Hands fumbled across Percival's backside. He sucked harder, resolved to stay focused.

Wetness enveloped his cock, an insistent tongue hugging while Bertram's mouth slid along his cock, momentarily causing him to forget his own task.

Bertram's chuckle reverberated through his core. Now he understood what the viscount had meant by losing one's sensibilities during the act.

Which only goaded him forward with more enthusiasm. He would make Bertram spend first.

He sucked harder, putting his weight on one hand so he could use the other to wrap around the base. He squeezed and pumped, sucked and licked in frantic determination. Beneath him, Bertram's thighs twitched and tightened, as his attention to Percival's prick waned.

With an upward thrust and a groan, Bertram loosed his seed into Percival's mouth. Percival gently squeezed his stones as he drank and swallowed.

Bertram roared a growl as he emerged from the bottom, flipping Percival onto his back and pulling his crotch to his face. Percival's squeal of surprise turned to laughter, then to sighs and encouragements as Bertram's wondrous mouth finished him off. His lover drank him down just as he had done for him.

Bertram plopped down by his side with a satisfied exhalation.

"That was positively magnificent," Percival said, exhaling heavily.

"Yes, yes it was." Drowsy contentment colored Bertram's words.

"Let's do it again sometime. Sometime soon."

Bertram pulled him into his arms and kissed his mouth, tangling his tongue with his, both tasting the other. He pulled away and brushed a damp lock from Percival's brow. "Percy, love, I'm humbled by your trust in me. I truly am."

Percival smiled as tears pooled on his lashes. Why had he denied himself such pleasure with his Bertie for so long?

CHAPTER TWENTY-ONE

The sun hung low on the horizon, painting the sky with streaks of
pink and orange. Paolo wrapped his arm around Barnaby's
shoulder.
"Join me on a new adventure?"
"With pleasure, my captain."
— *The Adventures of Paolo the Pirate Hunter*

Nice, late July 1879

Bertram leaned back against the wall of the window seat in
Percival's bedroom. He chuckled to himself. *Their* bedroom,
really. Of late, he only used his former bedroom as a grand
dressing room and closet. Armand always set out his clothes over
there. His dressing gown and nightshirt, however, were always laid
out on Percival's—*their* bed.

Another chuckle. Armand clung to some mode of propriety
where men wore nightshirts to bed, even if those men were young

lovers. He seemed to disregard the fact that both nightshirts remained untouched at the foot of the bed every morning.

Bertram tugged the curtain delineating the alcove, creating a small cocoon of space. Twilight quickly faded into night, stars slowing revealing themselves against the deep blue firmament. The day had been lazy and enjoyable. While Percival had gone into town, Bertram had retreated to the library. The discovery of a delightfully illustrated French edition of *The Count of Monte Cristo* by Alexandre Dumas made the afternoon fly by, something he hoped to achieve for readers of his own story one day.

After Percival's agent had sent along some promising prospects for London properties, the marquess had started purchasing objects to decorate this future London abode— paintings, porcelains, even fabrics for drapery and upholstery. Most everything had been delivered and presented to Bertram for his opinion. But not whatever it was Percival had gone into town for that day.

"It's just too precious. And I want to make sure it's perfect."

The curtains parted, and Percival entered. He took a seat on the opposite side. The vee at his dressing gown collar revealed he was, as was Bertram, nude under the striped silk robe.

"It's a lovely night."

Moonlight shimmered on the sea. "It is," Bertram agreed.

"We could go for a walk along the Promenade des Anglais."

Bertram eyed his lover. "We could."

"Or we could stay in."

"We are already dressed for that occasion."

Percival grinned. "Indeed." Suddenly, he lurched forward until he was at Bertram's side, one foot on the carpet, the other curled under him on the seat.

He reached into his pocket and drew out a small box. He placed it on his palm and presented it.

"For you, my dear Bertie."

Bertram's heart skipped a beat. He took the box and pulled off the lid.

In the center, couched in sumptuous red velvet and tied together with a thin red ribbon, were two gold rings. Masculine rings, each with an initial in a flourishing script.

Bertram delicately fingered the rings, inspecting the inscriptions. One had a *P*, the other a *B*.

"Percival and Bertram." He met Percival's beaming gaze.

"Yes." Percival flicked his hand. "Give it a try."

Bertram pulled an end of the ribbon, setting the rings free. He found his, with the *B*, and touched it to the tip of the fourth finger of his left hand.

"The little finger."

He repositioned the ring. The gold slid down the finger and nestled snugly at the base. "It fits perfectly."

"Of course it does. Our little fingers are the same size." Percival held up his left hand. "Remember?"

Bertram flushed at the memory of measuring hands before he'd pleasured them.

Percival put on his ring and admired it on his hand.

"This is what you went into town for today?"

"Yes. I've been planning this since your return."

"Are we now engaged, my lord?"

"Perhaps," he said with a grin. "Or perhaps it is just a little token to commemorate our travels, our journey together. We could, I suppose, be naughty and switch rings."

"I wear the *P* and you wear the *B*?"

Percival bit his lower lip, mischievousness arcing his brow. "Yes."

Bertram chuckled as his heart pounded a joyful beat. "May I kiss you, Percy darling?"

"The ring symbolizes my continuous and permanent permission for you to kiss me whenever you want."

"Whenever?"

"Yes. And wherever two men might properly kiss."

Bertram threaded his fingers through Percival's hair and drew him closer. "Such as right here?"

"With the moon and the stars as our witness."

Bertram nipped tenderly at his lover's lips, then pressed their mouths together. He swept his tongue inside before sucking Percival's, eliciting a whimper. The mere act of kissing could inflame him now. The prospect of kissing this man forever was pure euphoria.

Tears forced him to pull back and wipe his eyes. He leaned his forehead against Percival's. "I love you, Percy. I've loved you for so long. I will continue loving you for the rest of my life."

"I love you, too, Bertie. Thank you for waiting for my heart and for me to be ready."

The next morning

Percival unfolded the letter from Mother. She always had something pleasant to say, her letters the precise opposite of Father's usual berating. He glanced at Bertram, who looked positively engrossed in his letter, and happy about some news.

They sat closer together and on the same side of the mosaic table on the terrace these days. They shared the same view, and under the table touched knees and thighs.

"I just want to stay here forever." Percival sighed.

"You said that about Italy when we left."

"A villa in Italy would not be unwelcome either."

"And risk being the notorious duke abroad who never votes in Parliament."

Percival rumbled a distressed groan. "Please do not remind me of my future responsibilities."

Bertram grinned. "I count myself lucky I have none."

"Let's change the subject, shall we?" Percival set down the letter from Mother. "Once again, your news appears to be far more interesting than mine."

The grin widened. "Oh, I'm certain it is. Nicky is to be married."

"So the lady said yes."

"She did. And he would like me to be his groomsman."

"When and where is the happy event to take place?"

"London, early September." He scanned the letter. "He's put you on the guest list, but wants to know where to send the invitation." He met Percival's gaze. "I suppose he means here or in England. I confess I feel I should return to England as soon as I am packed to spend time with my cousin while he is still a bachelor." Sheepishness colored his expression. "I know this ends our time together a little sooner than you or I would have wanted. I don't want you to despise me for leaving." He glanced away. "And I don't know what our lives will be like once we return to normality in England."

It was now or never. Percival leaned forward, placing a hand on Bertram's forearm. "Come live with me."

"What? Live at Wood Hall?"

"No, no." Percival gave his lover's thigh a little swat. "In London."

A little crinkle of concern deepened above the bridge of Bertram's nose. "What about Oxford?"

"I'll take my exams during Michaelmas Term in October and be done with it all."

"Oh."

"You don't have a property in London, do you?" asked Percival.

"No. The Atherley house in town was sold long ago. Our notorious family debts, you know."

"Ah, yes, of course." Percival chuckled. "I'll lease the four bedroom. One bedroom for you, one for me. No one need know that we'll only sleep in one."

"We'll sleep in one..." Bertram echoed. "Are you propositioning me, my lord?"

"I am, my lord."

"All right. How do you propose we portray this to the outside world? Surely not as a love-nest."

"We're bachelors. Bachelors often live together until they are married."

"Except we'll never be married."

"Exactly," Percival said with a triumphant smile.

"I mean, we'll never be married to each other. In the meantime, Percy, you *will* have to bear the bonds of matrimony some time."

Percival ignored him. He poked a finger against Bertram's chest. "And to make it appear even more respectable, we'll invite your mother to stay with us for a few days."

"Certainly the presence of my mother will dispel any and all rumors of impropriety."

"And we'll get a dog." Percival nodded. "Dogs are symbols of fidelity."

Bertram seemed to be quelling amusement. "Our dog will be a symbol?"

"Like our rings."

"Dogs are not symbols, my dear friend," Bertram said with a laugh. "My mother has a dog. Winifred, a Blenheim spaniel. Wini is rather fussy and likes to bark. I'll tell Mama to bring Winifred when she visits. You can make your decision after that."

Percival beamed then leaned closer. "Will you say yes?"

"I will." Bertram threaded his fingers in Percival's hair. "Yes, I will live with you." He drew their faces together until their mouths almost touched, excited breath mingling with excited breath.

Percival's heart thrummed. "Let's always return here to France. For our anniversaries."

"Or Italy."

"Or Italy."

"Oh, absolutely." Bertram glanced sidelong at the view. "I think we should continue this celebration inside."

With a gleeful squeal, Percival ran through the terrace double doors. Bertram followed, closing the sheer curtains behind him.

The Harwell Heirs

Victorian aristocracy has very strict rules concerning marital connections and familial obligations. But the Harwell heirs—Helena, Sophia, and Arthur—discover love doesn't always follow the rules. Scandalous affairs force these scions of society to choose between duty and desire, deference and destiny.

Book 1: *The Pleasure Device*
Helena and Nicholas's story

Book 2: *Disobedience By Design*
Sophia and Joseph's – and Arthur and Joseph's – story

Book 3: *Where Destiny Plays*
Arthur and Lavinia's story

Book 4: *A Delicate Seduction*
Percival and Bertram's story

Book 5: *Discovering Her Delight*
William and Beatrice's story

Book 6: *Their Noble Deceit*
Percival, Bertram, Penelope, and Viola's story

More historical romance by Regina

Victorian
The Westerman Affair (Art & Discipline Book 1)
The Invitation (Art & Discipline Book 1.5)
Disputed Boundaries (Stories from the San Juan Islands)

American Revolution
The General's Wife: An American Revolutionary Tale
Winter Interlude: An American Revolutionary Novelette

About the Author

Regina Kammer is a librarian, an art historian, and an award-winning, international best-selling, multi-published writer of provocative historical romance and contemporary romance with a touch of history. Her short stories and novels make history sexier, whether the era is Roman, Byzantine, Viking, American Revolution, or Victorian. She's even sexed up contemporary settings, Steampunk, and Greco-Roman mythology. She has been published by Cleis Press, Go Deeper Press, Ellora's Cave, House of Erotica, Story Ink, Loose Id, The Naughty Literati, and her own imprint, Viridium Press. She began writing historical fiction with romantic elements during National Novel Writing Month 2006, switching to erotica when all her characters suddenly demanded to have sex.

Keep up with Regina
Check out her website: https://reginakammer.com/
Never miss a new release! Subscribe to *Kammerotica News*:
https://reginakammer.com/newsletter/